# DEADLY LITTLE GAMES

Also by Laurie Faria Stolarz

*Deadly Little Lies*
*Deadly Little Secret*
*Project 17*
*Bleed*
*Blue Is for Nightmares*
*White Is for Magic*
*Silver Is for Secrets*
*Red Is for Remembrance*
*Black Is for Beginnings*

# DEADLY LITTLE GAMES

A **TOUCH** NOVEL

*Laurie Faria Stolarz*

**HYPERION**

NEW YORK

First Hyperion paperback edition
10 9 8 7 6 5 4 3 2 1
V475-2873-0-11196
Printed in the United States of America
ISBN: 978-1-4231-3496-1
Visit www.hyperionteens.com

DEADLY LITTLE GAMES

# I

WHEN I CLOSE MY EYES I can picture his mouth. The way his top lip is slightly fuller than the bottom. The chapped skin on his lower lip. And how the corners of his mouth turn upward, even when he's trying to look serious.

My fingers completely saturated with clay, I continue to sculpt the image, remembering that night in front of my house, when I just knew he wanted to kiss me.

It was one of our last dates, and we were sitting in his car during that awkward moment when you're not exactly sure what happens next. Reaching to take my hand, Adam leaned in. My blood stirred, and my heart started pounding.

But I didn't kiss him.

I looked away, and his kiss barely grazed my cheek.

Is it possible that subconsciously I'm regretting that moment?

I open my eyes a couple of minutes later. My sculpture looks eerily real. I touch the chalky surface of the lips, almost able to feel his breath between my fingertips.

"Ten more minutes," Ms. Mazur announces, alerting us to the end of pottery class.

I clear my throat and sit back on my stool, wondering if the heat I feel is visible on my face. I glance around at the other students working away on their sculptures and suddenly feel self-conscious. Because all I've sculpted during this entire ninety-minute block is Adam's mouth.

Adam, who just happens to be my boyfriend Ben's biggest enemy.

Adam, who I'm no longer even interested in.

Adam, who despite the 300-plus other confusing reasons why I shouldn't be giving him a second thought, I've been thinking about all day.

I close my eyes again. The image of Adam's mouth is still alive in my mind—the way his lips were slightly parted that night, and the tiny scar that cuts across the bottom lip, maybe from when he fell as a kid. I try to imagine what he would say if he knew what I was doing.

Would he suspect that I was interested in him?

Would he think it was weird that I remembered so much detail about that moment?

Would he tell Ben what I was up to?

I take a deep breath and try my best to focus on the answers. But the only words that flash across my mind, the ones I can't seem to shake, don't address the questions at all.

"You deserve to die," I whisper, suddenly realizing that I've said the words aloud.

"*Excuse me?*" my friend Kimmie asks. She's sitting right beside me.

"Nothing." I try to shrug it off, adding a dimple to Adam's chin.

"Not *nothing*. You just told me that I deserve to be maggot feed."

"Not maggot feed, just—"

"Dead!" she snaps. Her pale blue eyes, outlined with thick black rings of eye pencil, widen in disbelief.

"Forget it," I say, glancing up at Ms. Mazur, sitting at her desk at the front of the room. "I don't know why I said that. Just daydreaming, I guess."

"Daydreaming about my death?"

"Forget it," I repeat.

"Are you sure you aren't still mad that I wouldn't let you borrow my vintage fishnet leggings?"

"More like I didn't *want* to borrow them," I say, taking note of her getup du jour: a fringed, fitted Roaring Twenties dress, and a couple of extra-long beaded necklaces that dangle onto the table.

"Even though they would've looked totally hot paired with that cable-knit sweater dress I made you buy. Still, it's no reason to say I deserve death."

"I'm sorry," I say, reluctant to get into it. Especially since the words remain pressed behind my eyes, like a flashing neon sign that makes my head ache.

"P.S.," Kimmie continues, nodding toward my

sculpture of Adam's lips, "the assignment was to sculpt something *exotic*, not *erotic*. Are you sure you weren't so busy wishing me dead that you just didn't hear right? Plus, if it was eroticism you were going for, how come there's no tongue wagging out of his mouth?"

"And what's so exotic about *your* piece?"

"Seriously, it doesn't get more exotic than leopard, particularly if that leopard is in the form of a swanky pair of kitten heels . . . but I thought I'd start out small."

"Right," I say, looking at her oblong ball of clay with what appears to be four legs, a golf-ball-size head, and a long, skinny tail attached.

"And, from the looks of your sculpture," she continues, adjusting the lace bandana in her pixie-cut dark hair, "I presume you're hankering for a Ben Burger right about now. The question *is*, will that burger come with a pickle on the side or between the buns?"

"You're so sick," I say, failing to mention that my sculpture isn't of Ben's mouth at all.

"Seriously? *You're* the one who's wishing me dead whilst fantasizing about your boyfriend's mouth. Tell me that doesn't rank high up on the sick-o-meter."

"I have to go," I say, throwing a plastic tarp over my work board.

"Should I be worried?"

"About what?"

"Acting manic and chanting about death?"

"I didn't chant."

"Are you kidding? For a second there I thought you

were singing the jingle to a commercial for roach killer: *You deserve to die! You deserve to die! You deserve to die!*"

"I have to go," I say again.

"Camelia, wait. You didn't answer my question."

But I don't turn back. Instead, I go up and tell Ms. Mazur I'm not feeling well and need to go to the nurse. Luckily, she doesn't argue. Even luckier is that I know just where to find Ben.

# AUDIO TRANSCRIPT 1

———

**DOCTOR:** I just pushed the record button. Shall we begin?

**PATIENT:** Let's get this over with.

**DOCTOR:** Why don't you start by telling me how your week is going?

**PATIENT:** My week sucks, just like every other week. Next question.

**DOCTOR:** Are you still having disturbing thoughts?

**PATIENT:** They don't disturb *me*.

**DOCTOR:** Let me rephrase, then. Are you still having thoughts of hurting yourself?

**PATIENT:** You know I was just joking about that.

**DOCTOR:** At least that's what you told me.

**PATIENT:** You believed it. If you thought I was actually capable of killing myself, you'd be required to lock me up. I know the rules.

**DOCTOR:** Why would you joke about something so serious?

**PATIENT:** Are you kidding? Feelings of depression, feeling sorry for myself, lack of self-esteem, eager for attention, craving some serious shock value . . . Shall I go on?

**DOCTOR:** No. Thank you.

**PATIENT:** Is this your first time as a therapist?

**DOCTOR:** Trying to insult me isn't the answer. I'm asking you an important question, and I'm not looking for a stock response. Why would you joke about killing yourself?

**PATIENT:** Boredom.

**DOCTOR:** I think there's more to it.

**PATIENT:** Okay, sometimes I get really pissed when I don't get what I want.

**DOCTOR:** And what *do* you want?

**PATIENT:** To stop coming to therapy sessions, for one.

**DOCTOR:** I don't make you come here. You must get something out of it.

**PATIENT:** I like to call it self-inflicted torture.

**DOCTOR:** There's the door. You can leave any time you want.

**PATIENT:** Is that what *you* want?

**DOCTOR:** No. I want to help you.

**PATIENT:** It's too late for that.

**DOCTOR:** Why do you say that?

**PATIENT:** Because people who have thoughts like mine can never go back. They can never be like regular people.

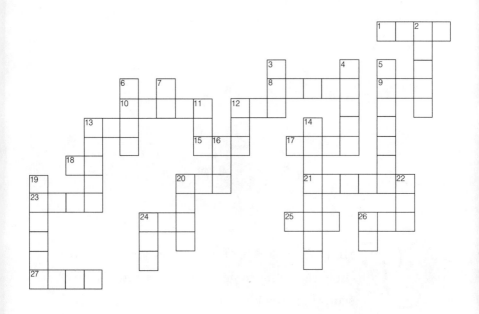

**Across**

**8.** I wear a _____ on my wrist, because it's only a matter of time.

**17.** I stabbed him in the _____.

**Down**

**20.** You made _____ bed, and now you'll have to lie in it.

## 2

*T*HE BELL RINGS JUST as I splash some water on my face, trying to get a grip. I tell myself that sculpting Adam's mouth was no big deal, and I've no reason to freak. But then why can't I shake this feeling that something's desperately wrong?

I hurry out of the bathroom, down the hallway, and into the gymnasium. No one's on the court yet. Most of the kids are probably in the locker rooms, changing into their sweats and sneakers.

But not Ben.

He has permission from Principal Snell to skip the actual "physical" part of phys ed class. Instead he's given the humiliating task of keeping score on the sidelines. Snell, along with most of the teachers at school, believes that Ben suffers from a fear of crowds, a fear that makes things like contact sports and switching classes with everyone else somewhat of a challenge for him. And so he's also been granted a License for Lateness—a pass that allows him to arrive at all his classes a few minutes behind everyone else, to avoid careening into people in the hallway.

The real reason that Ben avoids crowds is that he has psychometric abilities: abilities that enable him to sense things through touch. One might think having a power like that would make him want to touch people all the time—to find out all their dirty little secrets. But nothing could be further from the truth.

Almost three years ago, during a hike through the woods, Ben touched his girlfriend Julie's hand and sensed that she was cheating on him. Unable to control his need to sense more, he gripped her harder. Julie drew away, and though Ben tried to pull her back, she ended up tumbling backward off a cliff.

And dying almost instantly.

After that happened, Ben tried to avoid touch altogether. He dropped out of public school to be home-schooled by tutors, shut himself off from everyone he knew, and barely ventured outside his house. But then, a couple years later, he thought he'd try to have a somewhat normal life again and moved in with his aunt, two hours away, to enroll at our school.

That's when he accidentally touched me.

And everything changed.

Ben sensed that my life was in danger. And he was right. This past September, my ex-boyfriend Matt was plotting to take me captive in a twisted attempt to win me back. Then, just three weeks ago, Ben knew that someone was trying to deceive me. If it hadn't been for his keen awareness in both of those instances, I might not be here right now.

I wonder if he'll be able to sense that Adam's been on my mind, that I sculpted Adam's mouth, reminded of a kiss that didn't happen. And that just last night, when I couldn't fall sleep, I went down to the pottery studio in my basement and sculpted Adam's eyes, with the lids closed—the way he looked the instant before he tried to kiss me.

After a few minutes, boys start making an appearance on the basketball court for a little pregame, while girls sit up on the bleachers looking on.

A couple of minutes after that, Ben finally arrives.

As usual, he looks amazing. Dressed in layers of charcoal and black, his dark brown hair is rumpled to perfection, and his smile nearly steals my breath.

"Hey," he says, "what are you doing here? Aren't you supposed to be in class?"

"The nurse's office, actually," I say, flashing him my pass.

"Is everything okay?"

I nod, wondering if I'm overreacting. There's obviously nothing going on between Adam and me. But then why do I feel so guilty?

"Well, it's good to see you," he says. "But you know Muse won't let you stay."

"I know." Mr. Muse makes it his life's mission to suck the fun out of every sport imaginable, including those of

12

the romantic nature. "So, maybe I could just get a squeeze good-bye?"

"You bet," he says, coming closer. He smells like watermelon candy and the fumes from his bike. It's a scent I want to bottle up. And pour right over me.

Ben holds me close. His hands graze my lower back, igniting every inch of me. "Are you sure everything's all right?"

"I'm fine," I whisper, hating myself for lying to him.

"Because, you know you can tell me anything, right?"

"I know," I say, feeling worse by the moment.

Ben runs his fingers through the ends of my hair and breathes into the crook of my neck.

"I just wanted to see you," I whisper.

He takes a step back and looks into my face. His dark gray eyes are wide and searching. "How come I feel like you're not telling me everything?"

My pulse races, and my mouth goes dry. Meanwhile, the basketball makes a continuous slapping sound on the court behind us. I look over Ben's shoulder. All the boys are on the court playing basketball now. John Kenneally and Davis Miller, both notorious for giving Ben a hard time because of his history with Julie, pass the ball back and forth.

I do my best to ignore them, to ignore the echo of their shouting voices and the smack of the ball as it hits the backboard. But then Ben grips my hand tightly—until I almost have to pull away.

Only, before I can, he does. He takes a couple more steps back, letting go of my hand.

"Is something wrong?" I ask.

"Why don't *you* tell *me*?" He backs away even farther, as if he can't even stand being next to me now.

"Nothing's wrong," I blurt. "Everything's fine." I take a deep breath, my mind reeling. I struggle to think of something to say, just as a cluster of boys, en route to scoring a basket, plows right into Ben.

He falls hard, landing on his back with a grunt that makes me wince.

"Ben!" I hurry to his side, just as Mr. Muse finally shows up, ordering everyone out of the way.

Still, I stay with him. I try to take his hand again, but he pulls it away.

Meanwhile a smattering of snickers erupts behind me—from the pack of boys who collided with him.

"Just go," Ben says, avoiding my gaze.

"I'm not going anywhere. Not until I know that everything's okay."

"Go," he insists.

Mr. Muse demands that I leave, threatening me with a trip to Principal Snell's office. "Where are you supposed to be now, anyway?" he asks me. He helps Ben up and into a chair.

Meanwhile, I reluctantly head to the nurse—for real this time—because I truly feel like I'm going to be sick.

*I* SPEND THE REMAINDER of the block in the nurse's office before heading to the cafeteria for lunch, where Kimmie, Wes, and I sit at our usual spot by the exit.

"So, let me get this straight," Kimmie says. "You and Ben are fighting because you were fantasizing about macking with your ex?"

"Except, Adam isn't exactly my ex," I remind her. "We only went out a few times."

"But you still want his tongue in your mouth," Wes says, pointing at me with a sausage. He's stabbed the center with a plastic fork.

Wes has been our friend since freshman year. He's a fairly uncomplicated boy by day; most of his drama shows up at night. His dad, a former juicehead turned dickhead, hates the fact that Wes isn't "more dick, less chick"—he actually says that. He also calls him Wuss instead of Wes.

"You're sick," I tell him.

"But tasty." He takes a bite of sausage.

"At first I thought Ben's touch power was a bonus," Kimmie says. "But if he can read your mind on cue—learning about all your seedy fantasies—then maybe it's more of a drawback."

"First of all, I don't *have* any seedy fantasies," I tell them.

"Maybe that's your problem," Wes says.

"No," I say, correcting him. "My problem is that I'm thinking about Adam, and I don't want to be."

"You're not just *thinking* about him." Kimmie raises her ruby-studded eyebrow at me. "I thought those lips you sculpted in pottery class looked a little too luscious to be Ben's."

Wes leans forward and readjusts his wire-rimmed glasses. "What am I missing?" he asks, eager for the dirt.

"Three words," Kimmie says. "More. Random. Body parts."

"Except, that's four words," I say.

"Well, whatever." She rolls her eyes. "It's still significant. Not to mention creeptastic."

She's obviously comparing my sculpture of Adam's mouth to the one I did of Ben's arm a month ago, when I was trying to remember the branchlike scar that runs from his elbow to his wrist. A day or two after that, I sculpted Ben's eyes, as if they were peering at me through glass.

Both of those sculptures turned out to be premonitions.

Ben isn't the only one who's able to sense things through touch.

Over the past several months, instead of making my usual bowls and vases, I've been sculpting things from my future. First it was a car—the same one I spotted on the day Matt took me captive. Then there was the pinecone, which looked just like the air freshener that dangled from the rearview mirror of Matt's car. About a month ago it was a swordfish, similar to the wooden cutout affixed over the door of Finz restaurant, the place near where Debbie Marcus was hit by a car.

Debbie was a girl at school whose friends made it look like she was being stalked. They sent her creepy notes, making her believe that Ben (once on trial for the murder of his girlfriend on the cliff that day) wanted her to be Victim Number Two.

Debbie believed it, too. One night, on a walk home from a friend's house, anxious that Ben might've been following her, she wasn't really paying attention to where she was going and was struck by a car. The accident almost took her life.

When she came out of her coma two months later, even though Ben wasn't to blame, she was determined to make him pay—to make someone pay—for her lost time. And so she tried to frame him for stalking me in hopes that he would be forced to leave our school once and for all.

"Wait," Wes says. "Are you to imply that our dear Chameleon is once again having premonitions by way of pottery?"

"I'd appreciate it if you wouldn't call me reptilian names," I say.

"Would you prefer it if I called you a freak?"

"Plus," I say, failing to dignify his question with a response, "it hasn't *only* been body parts. What about the car, the swordfish, the pinecone?"

"Well, I still suspect something shady's going on," Kimmie says. "I mean, why Adam's mouth?—why not Ben's or your own? And why did it look all pouty, like he wanted a kiss?"

"There's more." I tell them about last night, how, when I couldn't sleep, I sculpted Adam's eyes.

"See?" Kimmie folds her arms. "More body parts."

"Whatever," I sigh, refusing to get into it again.

"Do you think you're sculpting this stuff and thinking about him because you miss him?" she asks.

"Or this could be your subconscious's way of trying to sabotage your love life," Wes suggests. "I saw something similar on *Love Rehab*."

Kimmie rolls her eyes—yet again—at the suggestion. She grabs a straw and attempts to blow the wrapper into Wes's recently overgrown yet still mousse-laden dark hair, but the wrapper fails to penetrate the hair's crusty outer surface. "Camelia hasn't even revealed the most disturbing piece in her jigsaw puzzle of a life," Kimmie says.

"Right," I say, knowing full well what she's talking about. "While I was sculpting Adam's mouth, I whispered the words 'You deserve to die.'"

"At me," Kimmie points out.

"More like, near you," I clarify. "It's not like I think *you* deserve to die."

"Then who?" Wes asks.

"No one. It's like someone put those words in my mouth—like the phrase got stuck in my head, and I couldn't let it go." I sink back in my seat, reminded of how sometimes, when I'm having one of my psychometric episodes—if I should even be calling it that—I'm able to hear voices.

About a month ago, I sculpted a horse kicking its legs up. It turned out to look just like the horse on the pendant that Ben gave to Julie shortly before she died. All the time I was sculpting the horse I kept hearing a voice in my head—a voice that told me to be careful.

The horse sculpture turned out to be a clue that someone was trying to trick me. That someone was Adam. Two years earlier, Adam (Ben's best friend at the time) had been dating Julie behind Ben's back. When Julie died, Adam, like everyone else, blamed Ben and wanted revenge.

And so last fall, when Adam learned that Ben had come to Freetown High seeking a somewhat mainstream life again, he secretly followed. Adam enrolled at the community college nearby and sought out Ben's love interest—me—as a way to make him jealous.

"So, what now?" Kimmie asks.

"Maybe you should give Adam a call," Wes says. "That is, if you don't wish him dead—in which case you should probably stay as far away from him as possible." He snatches my plastic utensils away. "I hear prison's a pain in the ass."

"No pun intended," Kimmie jokes.

"Well, naturally, I don't wish anyone dead," I say, as if the explanation were even necessary.

"Does Adam wish *you* were dead?" Kimmie asks.

"How would I know?"

"Maybe someone wishes Adam were dead." Wes scratches his chin in thought. "Or *maybe* you're supposed to save Adam, the way Ben saved you last fall. I mean, you did say you sculpted his eyes while they were closed . . . meaning, he could have been dead."

"Don't tell me this is going to be another semester of psycho notes, creepy photos, and cheap lingerie," Kimmie says, referring to some of the mysterious gifts I received when I was being stalked.

"Are you talking about Camelia's past with Matt, or your own colorful dating history?" Wes asks her.

"Jealous that I *have* a dating history?" She blows him a kiss.

"Maybe we're reading too much into things," I say, interrupting their banter.

"It's possible," Wes chirps. "Your verging-on-obsessive, shrineworthy stalkerazzi sculptures could very well be your subconscious's way of making it clear that you and Adam have some unresolved issues to attend to. And the twisted death-wish phrase could totally be chalked up to too many scary movies."

"Or too many detentions with Mr. Muse." Kimmie giggles. "My advice: give Adam a call. Be all casual, and ask him how he's doing."

"And if he's gotten any death threats lately," Wes adds.

I shake my head at the thought of contacting him again. It's not like we ended things on totally terrible terms. It's just that, despite how sorry he was afterward, despite the apologetic letters he sent asking for my forgiveness, what he did was downright cruel. "How am I supposed to explain to Ben that I'm calling his biggest enemy? . . . Someone I dated?"

"Who says he has to know?" Wes shrugs.

"He'll touch her and know, Einstein." Kimmie uses the knot of her beaded necklace to thwack him in the head.

"Well, if that's the case, I'm surprised you even lied to him in the first place," Wes says. "I mean, didn't you figure he'd know the truth anyway?"

"What can I say? I'm an idiot."

"Idiot or not, what you were sensing must have been pretty intense," Kimmie says. "I mean, to feel so guilty about it that you cut class, got a nurse's note, and willingly crashed Muse's phys ed block. So, you sculpted Adam's facial features. It doesn't exactly make you a two-timing tramp."

"And it doesn't exactly explain why Ben freaked out in gym class," Wes says. "Which brings us to the most obvious question: are you sure you aren't holding anything back from us? Might you have sculpted something a bit more scandalous than what you're actually admitting? A sexy little bowl or a naughty pot with a really curvaceous mouth?"

"Are there any other interesting body-part sculptures you want to tell us about?" Kimmie asks, playing along.

"No," I say, grateful for their humor—and for the fact that, despite this funked-up situation, they can actually get me to laugh.

"Is there any way to block what Ben is able to sense?" Wes asks. "Might a hint of garlic around your neck or chanting incantations under a waxing moon prove effective in warding off his abilities?"

"I doubt it." I smirk.

Kimmie reaches across the table to touch my arm in consolation. "Well, then, I hate to be the one to break it to you, but as far as Ben's concerned, it looks like honesty is your only option."

"A shame." Wes sighs, shaking his head in sympathy. "If only there could be some other way."

*I* GLANCE BACK AT BEN a couple of times in chemistry, waiting for him to look at me. Finally, he meets my eye, but it's only for a second.

Our teacher, Mr. Swenson, aka the Sweat-man, for obvious reasons, has got us pretty preoccupied today making snowflakes, using borax and pipe cleaners.

"These will have to sit overnight," the Sweat-man explains, "and then we can hang them in the windows."

"Doesn't he have enough flakes of his own?" Tate, my lab partner, nods toward the bits of dandruff sprinkled about the Sweat-man's shoulders and back.

But I'm too tense to laugh. As soon as Ben gets up to set his snowflake jar on one of the shelves in the back of the room, I follow suit, purposely crossing his path.

"We need to talk," I tell him.

He nods like he knows it's true.

23

I take a step closer, able to feel the sheer electricity between us. "How's your back, by the way?"

"Apparently a lot harder than the gym floor." He smiles slightly.

"So, everything's okay?" I ask, completely aware that the question is fully loaded.

"I don't know." His dark eyes soften. "Is it?"

I tuck a stray strand of hair behind my ear, knowing his question is loaded, too. But instead of unloading either of our questions, we make a plan to go to the Press & Grind after school.

Ben picks me up on his motorcycle, and I get on right behind him, holding him close, hugging his waist and wishing the ride could go on forever. But we're at the café in four minutes flat.

Ben orders a mocha latte for me and a large black coffee for himself, and then we sit in two cushy chairs toward the back—ironically, the same place where Adam and I sat on one of our dates.

Ben stirs his coffee, even though there's nothing in it, as if, maybe, he's every bit as nervous as me. "So, you have something you wanted to talk to me about?"

"I'm sure you already know. You were able to sense it, weren't you?"

"Just tell me," he insists, still focused on his stirring.

There's a good three minutes of silence before I can finally conjure up the nerve to tell him. "I've been thinking a lot about Adam," I say, my voice barely above a whisper.

"What about him?" He looks unfazed.

"You don't want to hear it. Just trust me when I say that it's you I want to be with."

"I *do* want to hear it." He looks up finally, making telling him the truth even harder for me.

I loosen my coat, but my face still feels hot. "I guess I've mostly been thinking about the way he looked," I venture.

"And about kissing him?" he asks, having obviously sensed the detail.

I look away, trying to avoid the question, remembering a kiss that Adam and I did once share. It was tiny and quick and happened sort of unexpectedly over a pizza and a pitcher of root beer.

"Camelia?" Ben says.

"I think he might be in trouble," I say, feeling a tunneling sensation inside my heart. I proceed to tell him about my sculptures and about how the words *you deserve to die* kept repeating in my mind.

"I guess we've never really talked too much about your power," he says.

"It's different from yours. It's like my mind locks on an idea, and I just start sculpting it. There's not even much creativity involved. It's as if I have no other choice but to get it out—the image fixed inside my head—whether I like it or not."

"And do you always hear voices when that happens?"

"Not always, but definitely sometimes, and I'm not the only one this happens to." I tell him about a blog I found a few weeks back. It was called Psychometrically Suzy, and the woman who wrote it talked about how one day, when she touched her father's old hat, she was able to hear his voice, even though he had long since passed away. "There are also people who are able to smell scents or experience certain tastes—all relevant to whatever they're touching," I continue.

"Sounds complicated."

"It is," I say, wishing things could be simpler. I reach out to take his hand, but he pulls away. "What's wrong?"

He shakes his head.

"Now it's your turn to be honest."

He takes a deep breath and lets it filter out slowly. "I sensed that you and Adam were together again."

"But we're not."

"But maybe you will be."

"Never," I whisper, reaching out to touch his hand again.

This time he lets me. His fingers close around my palm.

"This sculpture thing with Adam," I continue, "it's only happened a couple times. And maybe we're over-analyzing things. I was thinking that my sculptures could even be the result of a delayed response—premonitions that came too late. . . . I mean, it was only a few weeks ago that Adam and I were together."

"And what about the voice you heard, the *you deserve to die* message? If that's the result of psychometry—of something in your future—you can't just let it go."

"Yes, but it could be the same sort of thing. Maybe I was picking up on something from the past, something Debbie Marcus was thinking. This 'touch' stuff is new for me. I'm still trying to figure it all out."

"I couldn't bear to lose you." His dark gray eyes look wounded.

"You'll never lose me," I say, joining him in his chair. I rest my head against his chest and feel his heart beat. "We're meant to be together, remember?" I move to kiss him, but his lips are cold, still, brooding. And he doesn't try to kiss me back.

"I mean, what are the odds that we'd even meet?" I continue. "That two people with psychometric powers would ever find each other?"

Ben doesn't say anything. And we don't talk about Adam again for the rest of our time together. We actually don't say much at all. There's a tense silence between us.

A silence that we can't seem to fill even with small talk about school or our families.

A silence that gnaws away at the moment and prompts us to leave shortly afterward.

I SIT UP IN BED and switch on my night-table lamp. The street outside my window is barren and dark. I wish that Ben were here—that he would come and sit beside me on my bed, and that we could talk things through a bit more. Because I feel like we left so much unsaid.

I want to believe the excuses I told him earlier—all the logical reasons I've been so fixated on Adam. But I can't help thinking that maybe Wes and Kimmie were right. Maybe I *should* give Adam a call, if for no other reason than to safeguard myself from guilt. I wouldn't be able to forgive myself if something bad happened to him because I did nothing to try and stop it.

I glance at the clock. It's a little after eleven; Adam's probably still up. I reach for my cell phone and search for his number. With my finger positioned over the dial button, I stare back at myself in the dresser mirror.

I look the same as always: same loopy blond hair, same wide green eyes, same angular cheeks. But there's something about me that feels different now. Changed. And I'm not so sure I can ever change it back.

I close my eyes, still able to see the word *bitch* scribbled across the mirror, across my image, from when Matt broke into my room. I can hardly remember a time when things weren't so complicated, when a part of me wasn't afraid to fall asleep. Or when I felt completely certain about whom I could trust.

Finally, I push the dial button, eager to get this over with. The phone rings right away. At first I think his voice mail will pick up. But then I hear him answer. "Camelia?" he says. "Is it really you?"

"How are you?" I ask, trying to sound at ease. "I just wanted to call and check in . . . to see how everything's going."

"It's going better now," he says.

"So, nothing bad? No unhealthy relationships? No drama at school?"

"No. Definitely not. And hardly ever. Why?" He lowers his voice. "Is there something you're not telling me? Some ex-girlfriend of mine is telling everyone in town what a sexy playa I am?"

"Seriously?"

"I guess not," he says, seemingly disappointed. "But I'm not letting you off so easily. Did you hear something that I should know about?"

"No," I say, suddenly feeling more self-conscious than I ever thought possible.

"So, then, is this just an excuse you've devised to call me? Because, trust me when I say that you need no excuses. I love hearing from you."

"Hardly an excuse," I say, unable to stop the smile on my face. "I just wanted to check that all was good."

"Better than good. Ever since my temporary, though still painfully embarrassing bout of vengeance and stupidity, I'm a reformed man. And how about you? Is it safe to assume that life without me means you're no longer having a rough year?"

"I told you before: it's more like a rough life."

"Well, I've missed you . . . *and* your rough life."

I bite my lip, unsure how to respond, feeling a ten-pound pause drop on the line between us.

But then, "I'm really glad you called," he says. "I was afraid that I'd never hear from you again. I mean, I wouldn't blame you if that was the case. It's just—"

"Let's not rehash the past."

"Nope. No rehashing here."

"I'm just really glad to hear that things are going well."

"Wait, you're not getting ready to hang up on me, are you?" he asks. "We've only been talking for a couple minutes."

"Well, I don't really have much else to say."

"Are you kidding? The possibilities are endless. For starters, you could tell me that you'll call me again. Or, better yet, you could ask me out for coffee or a slice of pizza. Of course, letting me know that I can call you whenever I want is always a good possibility. Or, if you're feeling really generous, you could tell me that you miss me, too. I mean, I wouldn't even care if it was a lie."

"I should really get going," I say, holding myself back from letting out a laugh, and thinking how, maybe, in some tiny, totally platonic, just-a-friend-*ish* sort of way, I really do sort of miss him.

# AUDIO TRANSCRIPT 2

**DOCTOR:** So, how are things going? Are you getting along any better with your parents?

**PATIENT:** They think that as long as I'm not in prison or living on the street, all is well. I've even overheard my mother talking about me to her friends, bragging about how great I'm doing in school and how many friends I have. She's totally clueless . . . totally in denial.

**DOCTOR:** *Is* it denial? Or does she really believe those things about you?

**PATIENT:** One day I told her that I felt so alone it wouldn't even matter if I took my own life, because nobody would notice.

**DOCTOR:** And how did she respond?

**PATIENT:** She said I could try it, but then I wouldn't know if it was true or not because I'd already be dead.

**DOCTOR:** Were you serious about taking your own life, or just trying to get her attention?

**PATIENT:** Talking about death doesn't exactly make someone suicidal.

**DOCTOR:** Do you still feel alone?

**PATIENT:** All the time. Even when I'm with other people.

**DOCTOR:** Do *they* know that?

**PATIENT:** I don't think so. I can put on a pretty good show.

**DOCTOR:** And what's the benefit of that?

**PATIENT:** So they don't think I'm a freak, I guess. Sometimes I almost fool myself into believing that I'm someone else, that my life doesn't suck, and that I'm more like them.

**DOCTOR:** But if you're putting on shows all the time, how do you ever expect to get close to anyone, to let them in, and get to know the real you?

**PATIENT:** Simple. I don't.

**DOCTOR:** You don't ever want a true friend?

**PATIENT:** *Want* and *can have* are two very different things.

**DOCTOR:** Well, how about this? You *can have* what you *want* by getting rid of that alter ego of yours . . . by letting people get to know the real you.

**PATIENT:** No one would like the real me. If I ever want to be truly close to someone, it'll have to be by force.

**DOCTOR:** What do you mean?

**PATIENT:** I'll have to force them to love me.

**DOCTOR:** You can't force someone to love you.

**PATIENT:** That's *your* opinion.

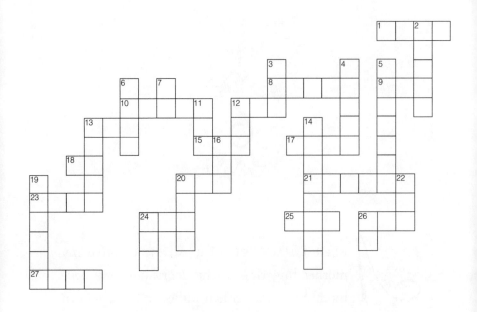

## Across

**9.** I spy with my little _____ someone
beginning with the letter A.

**10.** Opposite of having company.

**26.** You _____ so naive.

## Down

**2.** You are _____ far from my thoughts.

**14.** Stronger than observing.

**16.** Just _____ and me.

**19.** _____ and forever.

**26.** I _____ closer than you think.

6

*A*FTER I HANG UP with Adam, I notice my mother lingering in the doorway of my bedroom. She's got her hair pulled up. Her auburn corkscrew curls are piled high atop her head, adding at least four inches to her otherwise petite frame.

"Sorry I wasn't at dinner," she says. "I had to fill in for Ivy at the studio."

"The full-moon yoga class?"

She nods. "Lots of howling. My throat's still hoarse. Did you and Dad eat the raw-violi I left in the fridge?"

"Sort of. I mean, we considered eating it. It made its way onto the table. But we ended up having the rest of the rawkin' raw-sagna instead." (Rawkin' raw-sagna: a sorry excuse for real lasagna made with uncooked squash slices, tomatoes, and cashew paste, and served on—what else?— Elvis dinner plates.) I don't have the heart to tell her that Dad chucked both dinners and ordered us a pizza.

My mother grimaces, clearly on to my BS. She's what you'd call a health fanatic times one hundred, from the raw-ful cuisine she makes us eat to her handmade sanitary napkins (no joke: the woman actually uses kitchen sponges), and so, pepperoni-and-cheese-laden pizza ranks right up there with what fur coats are to PETA.

"Who were you talking to?" she asks.

"Adam."

"This late?"

"I just called to see how he's doing."

"I see." Her mouth twitches in irritation. "I thought you two weren't talking anymore."

"It was no big deal."

"This isn't going to be another semester of keeping secrets, Camelia, is it?"

I shake my head, thinking about the raw-sagna lie. "No secrets," I say, crossing my fingers behind my back, grateful that, at the very least, I don't have to lie about Ben anymore.

Initially, my mother wasn't so hot on the idea of me dating someone who was once on trial for the murder of his girlfriend. But, considering that he was acquitted, not to mention the fact that he saved my life not once, but three times, neither of my parents can deny that he truly has my best interests at heart.

"From now on, I'm telling you everything," I continue. Or at least as much as I think she can handle.

Mom nods, seemingly relieved, and then says she's planning a trip to Detroit to see her half sister. "It'll only be for a couple days. Your father will be home."

My aunt Alexia, labeled by her doctors as "a disturbed woman with suicidal tendencies, bouts of paranoia, and who claims to hear voices," has been in and out of mental institutions for as long as I've known her.

"Is she still at the hospital?" I ask.

"It's where she belongs." Mom closes her eyes and pauses for a breath, which is oddly apropos given the words embroidered on her T-shirt: TAKE YOUR TIME . . . AND TAKE MINDFUL KUNDALINI BREATHS.

"It'll be good to see her," Mom says. "Her doctors say she's making real strides and continuing with her art. Even if she's not completely expressive with her words, the doctors can look at her paintings and try to monitor her progress."

"When will you be going?"

"Next week. Friday."

I scooch back on my bed, wondering what it'd be like to talk with Aunt Alexia—to talk with someone who might understand what I'm actually going through. I glance at the journal on my night table, hoping my mom doesn't notice it. It's my aunt's, from when she was my age. I found it in the attic while putting away holiday decorations and have been reading it ever since. The journal documents my aunt's struggles with her illness. Though I'd be willing to bet it's more of a struggle with psychometry.

"Anyway, I'll let you know when I make the arrangements," Mom continues.

"Sounds good."

As soon as Mom says good night and leaves my room, I call Kimmie to give her the scoop about Adam.

"See, I told you," she says. "Don't you feel better now? You know he's okay."

"I guess."

"And so, maybe now that you two have talked, he'll stop occupying your thoughts, and *you'll* stop sculpting and chanting creepy things."

"Hopefully."

"And hopefully my dad will come to his senses and move back home."

"It's just a separation," I remind her. "Temporary."

"Tell *him* that. You should see his apartment in the city: lava lamps, beaded drapes, purple lights . . . and don't even get me started on his new karaoke machine. He made me listen to him sing 'A Hard Day's Night' by the Beatles more times than I'd like to remember. I'm still feeling a bit traumatized."

"Speaking of trauma, how's your mom?"

"A zombie, for the most part. But her good friends Jack and Daniel have been helping out."

"Seriously?"

"Not quite, but it's getting there. They partied last night at dinner."

"Define 'partied.'"

"She downed a glass before the Easy Mac was even on her plate."

"A glass doesn't exactly make a party."

"Unless that glass is more like a giant SpongeBob tumbler with a really long straw. She just keeps saying that my dad was the love of her life, that the two of them danced under the sea together at their high school prom, and that she can't imagine a life without him in it, blah, blah, blah. I really hate him for hurting her this way."

"I'm sorry," I say, for lack of better words.

"I know. It sucks. But life goes on, right?"

"Well, you know you can call or come over whenever you want."

"And I *will*," she says, perking up slightly. "You're my only friend with TiVo."

"And don't you forget it," I say, grateful that, though I can't bring her dad home, I can, hopefully, help cheer her up.

*A* FULL WEEK GOES BY without another thought about Adam. Until today.

It's after school, and I'm at Knead, the pottery shop where I work, showing Svetlana, my boss Spencer's new hire, how to make a pinch pot. The goal is for her to be able to help out in some of the children's classes, because she hasn't exactly been successful with any of the other responsibilities at the studio, as evidenced by all the broken greenware pieces, the constant shortages of the cash register, and the messy back room.

But her looks make up for or it, or so Spencer would insist, which I suspect is why he hired her in the first place. Standing at least six feet tall, Svetlana has long and flowing golden-brown hair, violet eyes, and boobs the size of boccie balls.

"Good?" she asks, holding out her sad little glob of clay, the shape of which reminds me of a toasted marshmallow.

There's a proud smile across her naturally pouting lips.

"Great," I lie, unable to burst her proverbial bubble.

"I make another one?" she asks, her Russian accent just as cute as she is.

"If you want," I say, feeling my own pinch pot begin to fold within my grip. I squeeze it into a ball and then wedge it out on my work board to get all the air pockets out. "Practice makes perfect, right?"

Svetlana nods and resumes her pinch-potting.

Meanwhile, I close my eyes, trying to will my Adam thoughts away. But they just keep on coming.

I roll out my clay ball, able to picture his shy little smile, the crinkles around his eyes, and the way he always used to hook his thumbs into his belt loops. I think back to the first time I met him, when he accidentally surprised me here at Knead. Weeks later, he told me how much he cared about me. And then he asked me to show him the wheel.

I remember how awkward it felt when he sat behind me on the stool, when he pressed himself against me, and then kissed the nape of my neck. I close my eyes, almost able to feel his fingers glide up and down the length of my arms.

"What are you making?" Svetlana asks, snatching me out of my daydream.

I open my eyes and manage a shrug; my face feels completely flushed. "I'm not really sure yet. Sometimes it's best to just go with your impulses—to see where inspiration takes you. It's good to remind students that, so they don't always feel pressured to produce something concrete."

Svetlana nods, but I'm not sure she gets it. Instead, she copies the shape I've got going. "Like snake, yes?"

"Yes," I say, rolling my snake up into a snail and giving it two long antennae that stretch wide, as if the snail were sensing something, too.

"So cute!" she raves, doing the same. "Good for kids."

I nod, happy she's happy, knowing that I probably haven't sculpted a snail since I was a kid myself. But for some reason, this is what my mound of clay wants to be. So, who am I to argue?

After work, Ben is waiting for me on his motorcycle, parked just outside the studio. Wearing dark sunglasses and a knowing grin, he looks just like a movie star.

And he kisses like one, too.

He revs his engine, and we drive off down the street, around the corner, and past Salt Marsh Beach. The sea air paints my skin and makes me feel more alive than ever.

Still, I wonder what Ben is feeling. He scoots forward a couple of times on his seat, as if the intensity between us is too much to bear. Maybe he's having a hard time concentrating on the road.

Or maybe he senses something else.

Once we get to my house, we find my parents in the living room. Mom's torturing Dad with a limb-tangling session of couples yoga, though it appears he almost enjoys it. He's lying on his back with his legs extended upward, and Mom's doing a back bend of sorts, while balancing on the balls of his feet.

Ben and I exchange pleasantries with them, forgoing my mom's less-than-tempting offer of compost parfaits, and then we head off to my room. Ben slips off his jacket and sits down on my bed. It's all I can do to hold myself back from joining him, but part of me is afraid of what he might sense.

I'm just about to ask him about the bike ride here—if, through two pairs of jeans, or the layer of his jacket, he was able to pick up on my Adam thoughts at the studio. But before I can, his hand falls on my aunt's journal, sticking out from beneath my pillow.

"What's this?" He runs his fingers over the faded red cover.

"It's my aunt Alexia's," I say, "from when she was our age."

He grasps the book harder, as if able to predict some of what's inside.

"My aunt and I have a lot in common, I think . . . with art and psychometry, I mean." I proceed to fill him in on some of the things that are detailed in the journal.

"Where is she now?" he asks.

"At a mental facility in Detroit. My mom's going to visit her this Friday. It'll only be for the weekend, but I was thinking about asking her if I could go, too. Maybe I could get a last-minute flight."

"I don't know. Two days without seeing you?" He

takes my hands and pulls me close. His kiss tastes like salt and honey.

I slide onto his lap and run my palms across his chest, but after only a couple of seconds he draws away. His breath is heavy and quick.

"Are you okay?" I ask, standing up from the bed.

Ben rebounds after a moment, but his whole demeanor's changed. "You were thinking about Adam again today, weren't you?"

I give a reluctant nod, wondering if I should tell him about the phone call. "But I didn't sculpt anything about him this time, so I'm thinking it was just a fluke."

"You're sure it isn't because you miss him?"

"Is that what you sense?"

Ben hesitates, staring into my eyes as if trying to read something there. "I trust you," he says finally.

"Good, because you're the one that I miss."

"But I'm right here."

I move onto his lap again, my legs crossed behind his back. I close my eyes and picture us on his motorcycle, riding down the sunny beach strip, the seat pressing against the backs of my thighs and urging me closer to him.

We kiss for several minutes, until I feel him pull away once more. "I think I should probably go," he says.

"Why?" I ask, giving him some space. I move off his lap and get up from the bed. "What's wrong?"

"I should be asking you the same."

I shake my head, feeling a lump form in my throat.

Ben looks away, clearly disappointed, as if he knows

I'm keeping secrets. "On second thought, why don't you go to Michigan with your mom? Some time away might be good for you. It might be good for both of us."

"Wait, what are you saying?"

"I'm saying that I have to go." He stands and pulls on his jacket.

"Ben—no. Let's talk about this."

"Maybe tomorrow," he says, visibly shaken.

I'm shaken, too, not quite sure what just happened. Or how I can undo it.

8

*A*FTER THE INCIDENT with Ben, I head over to Kimmie's to cry on her shoulder. We're sitting in her bedroom, amid rolls of pink taffeta and leopard-print spandex, as she works on one of her latest designs. It's Kimmie's goal in life to have her own clothing line one day. She's even taken some weekend workshops at the Fashion Institute in an effort to develop her inner fashionista.

"I call this dress Ballerina Meets Bad Girl," she says, tearing the hem of a skirt to give it a tattered edge. "Your honest opinion: do you think a whip is too much as an accessory? Because a whip would look totally cute if it had a pink handle."

"Maybe just a smidge," I say, flopping back on her bed, accidentally landing on a bag of feathers.

"You're really upset, aren't you?" She sets down her pinking shears.

"How can I not be?"

"Right," she says, handing me a tissue. "But I vaguely recall mentioning something about how honesty is your only real choice where Ben's concerned."

"Maybe now's not the best time to be saying, 'I told you so.' Plus, it's not like I intentionally lied to him. I mean, yes, Ben's my boyfriend, but I'm still my own person. Aren't I allowed to keep anything to myself?"

"Not when you're fantasizing about your ex while dating a mind reader."

"He's not exactly a mind reader," I say, correcting her. "And I'm not exactly fantasizing."

"Okay, then, having kinky thoughts." She rolls her eyes, as if annoyed that I'm nitpicking over words. "Try to think of Ben's gift as a small sacrifice. I mean, let's face it, the boy *does* look pretty smokin' on that motorcycle of his."

"That's totally beside the point," I say, still unable to disagree.

"You need to see things from his perspective," she continues, "because this must be really hard for him. There are just some things you don't want to know about your main squeezie. Like, I once dated this guy who said that he sometimes liked to floss his teeth and examine the findings under a microscope. Now, tell me, did I seriously need to know that?"

"Did *I* seriously need to know it?" I ask, all but gagging at the image. "But I don't think Ben's power is all that random. I mean, some of what he senses can be sort of unpredictable."

"No pun intended," she jokes.

"But for the most part, it's the intense stuff—the stuff at the forefront of people's minds."

"The stuff we like to hide," Kimmie says.

I nod, grateful for her friendship, and for the fact that I never feel like I have to hide anything with her. She and I have been through it all: from Barbie-and-Ken breakups and hard-wire braces to the time when Billy Horton, my longtime crush and first-time kiss, told the entire freshman class that said kiss tasted like sweaty socks.

"Do you think it's possible to be attracted to someone and not even know it?" I venture.

"Meaning you're Adam-curious?"

"*No.*" I shake my head at how ridiculous the idea sounds outside my head.

"Might there be any residual sparks left between the two of you?" She shoots me an evil grin.

"That's just it; there never were sparks. Adam's a nice guy, but I never really felt that way about him."

"So, then, why do you keep thinking about him now?"

"The million dollar question," I say, grabbing a furry pillow off her bed and hugging it to my middle. "I just don't want to jeopardize things with Ben."

"Give yourself a break, Chameleon." She passes me a half-eaten bag of candy corn, kept conveniently on her night table. "You can't help your thoughts. I mean, seriously, if anyone could read my thoughts, I'd probably be locked up."

I pop a couple of candy corns into my mouth, somehow already feeling a smidge better.

"The way I see it," she continues, "it basically comes down to a matter of trust. He has to trust you, but you can't go giving him reasons not to."

"Do you realize that's probably the wisest thing you've ever said to me?"

"Even wiser than my teeth-flossing analogy?" She smiles, her newly acquired lip ring clinking against her front tooth. "Bottom line: I bet this whole thing with Ben will blow over, especially since you didn't think about Adam for a full week. I mean, a few random thoughts while you're at work—"

"Plus, I didn't sculpt anything about him."

"Exactly," she says. "Not to mention that you didn't hear voices this time, or chant anything psycho."

"But then, if my Adam thoughts were so completely random and meaningless, why did Ben pick up on them right away?"

"Because you're feeling guilty. Ben's sensing that guilt, which is the precise reason you need to be honest with him. The more truthful you are, the less shady you'll feel."

"Wow," I say, slightly reassured. "You're like an expert on all this stuff."

"I'm an expert on a lot of things," she says with a snip of spandex.

"So, then, what if this stuff with Ben *doesn't* blow over?"

"Find another squeezie?"

"I'm serious," I say. "I don't want to lose him."

"Then maybe you *should* go away for a little bit. After all, absence makes the heart grow horny, right?"

"That's not exactly how the saying goes."

"But it should, because you know it's true. If you go away for a couple of days, Ben won't know what to do with himself."

"Maybe you're right," I say, tossing more candy corn into my mouth (therapy in a bag).

"Damn straight, I am. Now, the bigger question: can I fit into your suitcase? Because I really don't feel like staying here by myself."

"But you're not by yourself. You have Nate, remember?"

"Annoying little brothers don't count."

"But that annoying little brother really needs you right now."

"Because my mom is pretty useless. Did I tell you? The woman even went looking for a job today; that's why she's not home. I mean, honestly, do they offer jobs to people whose past sixteen years of experience include making pancakes, folding laundry, and taxiing kids around all day?"

"Yes; they call them nannies."

"She belongs at home," Kimmie insists. "Not looking around for minimum-wage jobs."

"Since when do you believe in a 1950s lifestyle?"

"Since my mother started making a complete and utter fool of herself."

I bite my tongue, reminding myself that Kimmie's world has been knocked on its side, that she obviously isn't used to the idea of her mom's not being at her beck and call, and that she probably doesn't have the best perspective right now. "Maybe finding work will help your mom," I venture. "It could help get her mind off your dad."

Kimmie yanks the hem of her fabric, producing a gaping tear. A second later, there's a knock on her bedroom door. "What do you want?" she calls out.

The door creaks open. It's her eight-year-old brother, Nate, Legoland T-shirt and all. "Mom still isn't home yet," he says to Kimmie, "and I'm hungry. Can you make me a grilled-cheese?"

"See?" Kimmie says with another rip. "Already I'm picking up her slack."

Later, at home, I head into the kitchen, where my dad is picking up his own slack. He's doing some work at the kitchen island, having taken a few days off from his tax-attorney duties to spend some extra time with Mom before her trip. He'd wanted to accompany her, but both of them knew it'd be smarter for him to stay home.

In other words, neither of them trusts me.

And who can really blame them?

The last time they both went away together, a stalker broke into our house, our basement turned into a scene out of *Fright Night*, and I nearly gave my boyfriend a concussion.

"Hey, there," Dad says, pausing from his papers to look up at me. He takes off his wiry glasses and rubs his overworked eyes.

Mom is in the kitchen, too, whipping up a batch of no-bake fudge.

"Hey," I say, taking a seat on an island stool. "Did anyone call for me?"

"Your dad and I had a *great* day; thanks for asking." Mom smirks.

"How was your day? Did anyone call for me?" I smile.

She dumps a gob of coconut oil into her raw-ful mixture. "*Anyone* meaning Ben?"

"Am I that transparent?"

"It's just that I was sixteen once, too."

"Right," I say, shuddering even to think of her pre-forty—pre-me, pre-Dad, when it was just her hippie self, burning incense, going braless, and dating poets.

"Sorry, honey, but it's been pretty quiet around here," she says. "How was Kimmie's?"

"Utterly depressing, but still thoroughly mind-clearing."

Mom stops pureeing to look up at me. "Care to elaborate?"

"Care to let me go to Detroit with you?"

Dad's staring at me as well. "That was rather blunt."

"You guys said you wanted brutal honesty."

"I think we're just a little surprised," Mom says. "I mean, where did all of this come from?"

"I don't know." I shrug. "I just thought it might be a good time for me to visit with Aunt Alexia. To get some perspective. To get away for a couple days."

"That's all it will be, you know," Mom says. "A couple of days. I need to get back here for work."

"I know that," I say, surprised that she's even entertaining the idea.

"And you know that your mother will be busy for most of the trip," Dad adds. "She and her sister have a lot to talk about."

I nod, watching as Mom continues to mix her cocoa-nib concoction. Her forehead furrows with what I imagine to be deep and thoughtful concentration.

Meanwhile, Dad's eyes remain fixed on mine, perhaps trying to figure me out. "Well, we'd have to try and get you a last-minute ticket," he says.

"But why not?" Mom continues. She moves to give Dad a hug from behind. "It'll be nice to have the company."

"*Seriously?*" I ask.

"Why not?" she repeats, sliding the bowl of fudge batter toward me.

I eat the gritty goodness by the spoonful, almost surprised at how easy it was to persuade them. And how yummy raw honesty can be.

*A*FTER SCHOOL THE following day, Kimmie and Wes come over to help me pack. We're sitting in my bedroom, pulling apart my entire wardrobe in search of what Kimmie deems "travel-ready."

Wes sniffs the underarm of one of my cashmere sweaters and then snuggles the fabric against his cheek. "What's the weather in Detroit these days?"

"Who cares about weather?" Kimmie makes a face at an old pair of gaucho pants lingering at the back of my closet. "Make sure you don't say anything wacko. No chanting, no death threats, and definitely no references to hearing voices of any kind."

"Or else you might wind up a fellow patient at Happy Acres, rather than just a visitor," Wes says.

"Not funny," I tell him. "And, for your information, the facility is called Ledgewood House."

"Has Ben called to say good-bye?" he asks.

"*Ix-nay* on the *en-talk-bay*," Kimmie says. "Definitely a sore subject."

"It's fine." I sigh. "Ben and I are having issues. It happens. Life goes on. Isn't that your motto?"

"It is," she says, stuffing the zebra-print shrug she bought me last Christmas into my bag. "And, like me, you're full of crap."

"Well, hopefully a couple of days away will make me less full of crap and more full of answers."

When I saw Ben in school earlier, I filled him in on the fact that my parents had agreed to let me go to Detroit. I told him I'd miss him, and I thought he would've said the same.

But he didn't.

He merely wished me good luck and said he'd see me when I got back.

"You *could* call him," Wes suggests. "Why be a spectator in the game of love? Take charge. Don't wait around and let the boy call all the shots."

"As cheesy as all of that sounds," Kimmie adds.

"Cheese or not, I know what I'm talking about." He sulks. "I've lived it. I've learned it."

Kimmie lets out a laugh. "With who, Romeo? That Wendy girl you paid to date you?"

It's true. Wes, desperate to get his dad off his not-so-studly back, once paid a random college girl to pose as his girlfriend. It worked out well for a while, but then the less-than-happy couple "broke up" over irreconcilable differences of the financial kind.

"Oh, and because I don't have a dating history as big as your mouth, it doesn't quite measure up?" he asks.

"I hate to break this to you, but that isn't the only thing of yours that doesn't measure up." She waggles her pinkie at him.

"Wouldn't you like to know?" He grins.

"I think I'm all set," I interrupt, zipping up my bag.

"Don't forget this." Still cuddling my sweater, Wes purrs a couple of times before tossing it my way.

"Yeah, I can't imagine *why* your dad thinks of you as feminine," Kimmie mocks.

"Not feminine. Just appreciative of fine fabrics. There's a difference."

"So right," she says, calling for a silent truce.

They give me a hug before heading out. Afterward, I lie in bed, tempted to take Wes's advice and give Ben a call. I reach for the phone and dial his number, but then click it off just shy of the last digit. Because maybe talking to him isn't the best answer right now. But maybe taking a little break is.

# AUDIO TRANSCRIPT 3

**DOCTOR:** So, I wanted to ask you about something that came up during our last session. What did you mean when you said that you can force someone to love you?

**PATIENT:** I meant just what I said: if you want someone badly enough, you can make them yours.

**DOCTOR:** Even if they don't want to be with you?

**PATIENT:** Sure.

**DOCTOR:** Have you ever tried?

**PATIENT:** Not yet.

**DOCTOR:** Do you plan to try?

**PATIENT:** I don't know. *(Patient laughs.)*

**DOCTOR:** Why is that funny?

**PATIENT:** This whole conversation's funny.

**DOCTOR:** Forcing someone to do something they don't want to is hardly amusing . . . at least, not to me.

**PATIENT:** Sometimes people don't know what they want. Sometimes they need to suffer a little to understand what's really good for them.

**DOCTOR:** Did that work in your case?

**PATIENT:** What do you mean?

**DOCTOR:** Did the suffering your father made you endure help you to see what you truly wanted?

**PATIENT:** It helped me to see what I *don't* want.

**DOCTOR:** So, what makes you think that forcing someone to do something against his or her will won't have the same effect that it did on you?

**PATIENT:** *(Patient doesn't respond.)*

**DOCTOR:** Do you want to talk about your suffering?

**PATIENT:** There's not too much to talk about. My father used to beat me. My mother looked the other way.

**DOCTOR:** And now?

**PATIENT:** Now I don't really see my father anymore. And my mother basically ignores me.

**DOCTOR:** So, where does that leave you?

**PATIENT:** Pretty messed up, I guess. *(Patient laughs.)*

**DOCTOR:** You're laughing again.

**PATIENT:** Sorry, I just think this whole scenario is pretty funny.

**DOCTOR:** How so?

**PATIENT:** I mean, if anyone actually knew what I've got going on inside my brain . . .

**DOCTOR:** Care to enlighten me?

**PATIENT:** Not really. You'll just have to wait and see, like everybody else.

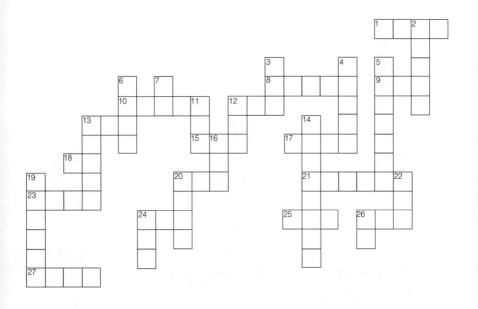

## Across

**18.** I am alone. There's only _____.

**20.** Sometimes I truly hate _____.

**23.** When he _____, I cut out his tongue.

## Down

**3.** A couple minus _____ = no one.

## IO

*O*NCE WE LAND IN Detroit, instead of checking in at our bed-and-breakfast first, we get a rental car and drive straight to the facility where Aunt Alexia is staying. It's after nine, so I'm thinking visiting hours are over for the day, but Mom insists that because we're family we have every right to see her right away.

The facility is nothing like what I imagined—ironically, it's more like a funeral home, a place to bring the dead, than a place to keep the suicidal from dying. We pull up in front of a long brick walkway that leads to a giant white house. Spotlights and a lamppost illuminate the area, but there's no sign out front, and all the window shades are drawn. Mom puts the car in park, and we head to the main entrance.

An older woman greets us, introducing herself as Ms. Connolly, the head nurse. She invites us inside, and the funeral-home vibe persists—mahogany woodwork, shelves full of old and dusty books, and antique-looking furniture.

"It's uncanny," Ms. Connolly says, giving me the once-over. "You look just like your aunt. If I didn't know better, I'd say you could almost be sisters."

"Can we see Alexia?" Mom asks, wanting to avoid the small talk. Her hands are shaking, and she can't stop fussing with her scarf. And suddenly I'm nervous, too.

"I'm sorry," Ms. Connolly says. "But Alexia had a tough day today and she was put to bed after dinner."

"What does that mean?" Mom asks.

"She was given a little something to help her sleep," Ms. Connolly explains.

"But I don't understand. She knew we were coming."

The woman nods. Her beady black eyes narrow, and she sucks in her lips, making the truth pretty apparent— that it's *because* of our visit that Aunt Alexia's day was rough.

"I see," Mom says, clenching her teeth.

Ms. Connolly musters an encouraging smile. "I'm sure she'll be more prepared to see you tomorrow morning."

Mom spends another good fifteen minutes or so continuing to try to get us in, but Ms. Connolly doesn't cave. She doesn't even flinch.

Meanwhile, a female voice screeches from down the hallway: "I want my pillow! Just give me my goddamned pillow!" At the same moment, something smacks against the hallway door with a loud, hard crash that makes me jump.

Definitely our cue to leave.

Mom drives us to our B and B for the night. I try to get her to talk about stuff—about how frustrating the situation is and how stressed Aunt Alexia must be. But Mom doesn't want to hear any of it. Instead she takes what would have to be the longest shower in the history of water, and then heads straight to bed with barely a good night, never mind her nightly sun salutations.

Before I go to bed myself, I check my phone for messages. I have one missed call from Ben. It seems he phoned just before I boarded the plane, but he didn't leave a message.

Part of me wonders if it was to wish me well once again. Another part secretly hopes that it was to ask me not to go. I'm tempted to call him back to find out the answer. But I follow my mother's lead instead, and drift off to sleep.

After breakfast the following morning, Mom and I head straight to the hospital to see Aunt Alexia. This time we're allowed to stay. There's actually a meeting set up for Mom, Aunt Alexia, and her doctor. Mom asks me if I want to wait in the lobby, but the thought of sitting amid all that funeral-home decor, coupled with the threat of hearing someone screech about her missing pillow, is far more unsettling than the idea of spending the morning by myself in an unfamiliar city. And so I take Ms. Connolly's advice and head to the strip mall down the road.

A couple of hours later, Mom and I meet up for lunch at a nearby coffee shop.

"So, how was it?" I ask her.

"Good." She actually smiles—the first smile I've seen on her in days. "Her doctor asked me some stuff about our childhood, so I got to tell my side of things."

"Did Aunt Alexia tell hers?"

Mom shakes her head. "She mostly just listened. But that's okay, too. Because at least she knows how sorry I am."

"Even though it wasn't your fault."

My mom nods, but I'm not sure she believes it. Growing up, Aunt Alexia was hated by their mother— my grandmother. According to Aunt Alexia's diary, and confirmed by a few details from Mom, my grandmother blamed Aunt Alexia's birth as the reason her husband left them. Meanwhile, my mom was loved and indulged, often as a way to make Aunt Alexia jealous.

"She really wants to see you," Mom says.

I take a bite of scone, thinking back to the last time I saw Aunt Alexia—probably when I was around seven or eight. She came to visit for the holidays, but then left on the afternoon of Christmas Eve.

I remember how nervous she was—always looking over her shoulder, forever checking out the window and fussing with her hair. And I remember all the art supplies she brought along. I wanted her to teach me what she knew, wanted to be able to do brushstrokes just like hers, but Aunt Alexia wouldn't let me join in, insisting that art was for bad girls, and that I was better off playing with my dolls.

She left soon after, even though Mom begged her to

stay. She just kept saying that she needed to get home for an interview she'd forgotten about. Finally, Mom caved and drove her to the train station.

We got a call from the local hospital a few hours later. Aunt Alexia never got on her train. Instead she ended up at the motel in the next town over, where she tried to kill herself, using some telephone cord to hang herself in the shower. Another guest at the motel had heard some weird noises coming from her room and asked the manager to check things out. That's when they found Aunt Alexia, thankfully in time to save her.

"Just think about it," Mom says to me. "No pressure."

"I want to see her. That's why I'm here."

Mom reaches across the table to squeeze my hand. "When I brought up your name, she said she remembered how much you liked to watch her paint. I told her that you were an artist as well, and she asked if you'd like to see some of her work."

"She wasn't upset?"

"Why would she be?"

I shrug, still wondering what Aunt Alexia meant years ago when she told me that art was for bad girls. Was it a lame attempt to try to get me interested in other things? Was she afraid that I might end up like her?

"When can I see her?" I ask.

"How about after lunch? We leave tomorrow, so we need to take advantage of every moment."

"Sounds good," I say, eager to find out some answers.

# II

*B*ACK INSIDE THE FACILITY, Mom explains that this is an alternative place, that they give the patients a lot of liberties that bigger facilities don't.

"For example?" I ask, closing the door behind us.

Before she can answer, Ms. Connolly appears. She ushers us through the lobby and into an art studio, as if things have all been arranged. "This is the art therapy room," Ms. Connolly says, opening the door wide.

The ceilings are high. The smell of turpentine is thick in the air. And the room is set up with easels, drop cloths, and the requisite bowl of wax fruit as a centerpiece to paint (only, unlike the wax-fruit arrangement at school, this one has a bite out of one of the apples).

I continue to look around, finally noticing that we're not alone, that someone's working in the corner, only partially obscured by a canvas.

It's Aunt Alexia. I'd recognize her anywhere. She has long and wavy pale blond hair and wide green eyes that stare in our direction.

"Do you want to come and say hello?" Ms. Connolly asks her.

Alexia takes a couple of steps toward us. She's much tinier than I remember. She's only a few years younger than my mother, and yet she almost looks like a little girl. Her outfit—a cotton dress with billowing sleeves—drapes her body, almost like a drop cloth itself.

"Do you remember me?" she asks. The angles of her cheeks are sharp, and her mouth looks like a tiny pink seashell.

I nod, and she comes closer. "You're an artist, your mother tells me."

"Well, I'm not really sure I'd go that far."

"You're an artist," she repeats, nearly cutting me off. Her voice is like tinkling wind chimes.

"I was telling Aunt Alexia about your pottery," Mom explains.

Alexia wipes her paint-covered fingers on the front of her apron, producing a bright red smear that makes it look as if she were bleeding from the chest. She extends her hand for me to shake. I try to let go after a couple of seconds, but instead she pulls me across the room toward her canvas, eager to show me her work.

"I've been waiting to get your opinion on this one," she says, picking a canvas up off the floor. She turns it over so I can see.

It's a painting of a boy, with an undeniable resemblance to Adam—same wavy brown hair, same olive skin. Dark brown eyes, dimple in his chin, scar on his lower lip.

"Interesting, isn't it?" she says, checking for my reaction.

I swallow hard, not quite knowing how to respond.

"I painted it yesterday," she continues. "When I heard you were coming, I went to my photo album and took out a picture of you—one that your mother had recently sent me. I touched the photo, and the image of this boy popped into my head." She nods toward the painting. "Has that ever happened to you?"

Instead of answering, I glance at my mother. She wipes her eyes with a tissue, perhaps moved to see that Aunt Alexia and I have something in common.

If only she knew how much.

"I was hoping to show this to you last night," Aunt Alexia explains, "when you first arrived. But unfortunately, things got a little detoured the further I got into my work."

"Oh," I say, wondering what *detoured* means, exactly, and if that's the reason she was *put to bed*.

"Do you remember the last time I came to visit you?" she asks, narrowing her eyes, as if trying to read my mind. "We never did get to paint together, did we?"

"No," I whisper, and look away.

"So, would you like to paint together now?" She looks to my mother for approval.

"It's up to Camelia," Mom says.

"I'm not really much of a painter," I say, for lack of a better excuse.

"It's easy when you use your hands." She flashes me her paint-stained palms. "You use your hands with sculpture, too, right?"

"I suppose."

"Well, you have to admit, there's nothing quite like sinking your fingers into your work—becoming one with what you create . . . with what you touch."

"Your mother and I will stay in the studio as well," Ms. Connolly assures me.

I take a deep breath, thoroughly confused. But then I look toward the portrait of Adam again, and know that I have no other choice.

12

*W*HILE MOM AND MS. Connolly look on from the doorway, I slip into a paint-splattered smock, feeling my insides rattle.

"Relax," Aunt Alexia says, obviously sensing my hesitation. She hands me a paint-covered palette and then places a fresh canvas on her easel.

"So, what should we paint?" I ask, eager to know how this is going to work.

"Why don't we just see where our painting takes us?" she says. "There's no sense forcing a picture that doesn't want to be, right?"

I nod, taken aback by how much she thinks like me.

She dips her finger into the black paint and I do the same. Together, we create a spiral shape on the canvas. Aunt Alexia uses her middle finger to apply the brown paint, adding tonality to the individual rings. It's amazing to watch her work, to see how much detail she can convey simply by using the tips of her fingers.

After several minutes, Ms. Connolly excuses herself, but my mother remains. Mom pulls up a stool and flips open a magazine.

"You're very talented," Aunt Alexia tells me. "A natural."

I feel my face flush, wondering if she's just being patronizing about my swirls and smudges, but her expression seems sincere. Our fingers completely covered in acrylics, Aunt Alexia and I paint a giant, diamond-shaped border. Inside it we paint a snail, the shell of which is almost iridescent, in shades of silver and blue.

"And now for the finishing touch." Aunt Alexia dips her finger back into the black, and paints two long antennae that extend outward. She looks back at me with a menacing grin, as if she knows something I don't.

I'm just about to ask her what it is, but then I figure it out: it's just like the snail I sculpted at Knead, when I was showing Svetlana how to make a pinch pot, when I was thinking about Adam.

I take a step back and drop my palette. It lands against the floor with a thud. I look to see Aunt Alexia's response, but she's sitting on a stool now, rocking back and forth and covering her ears with her hands. She whispers something that I can't quite make out.

"Aunt Alexia?" I ask.

"You deserve to die," she whispers.

I shake my head, hoping I've heard her wrong.

"Camelia?" Mom says, standing up from her stool.

"You deserve to die!" Aunt Alexia shouts, staring right

at me. Her eyes are wild, and her teeth are clenched.

I move toward my mother, who's already called for help.

"No!" Aunt Alexia screams, shaking her head. Black paint stains her cheeks and neck.

A second later, two nurses rush in to restrain her. Aunt Alexia puts up a fight, kicking, screaming, and trying to bite her way free. The easel falls over with a crash.

"What happened?" Mom asks, all but covering her own ears, too. "Why would she say that?"

But I know my aunt doesn't really wish me dead. I know she must be hearing voices—most likely the same voice that played in my head back when I was sculpting Adam's mouth in pottery class.

Alexia elbows one of the nurses in the eye. Together, the nurses eventually wrestle her to the floor, pinning her arms behind her back and sitting on her legs so she can no longer kick. The nurse that got elbowed takes a needle from her pocket and jabs it into Alexia's arm. It settles her right down.

Her eyes go blank. Her body turns limp. And she's dragged away. Meanwhile, Mom wraps her arms around me, telling me over and over again how sorry she is.

Ms. Connolly comes to apologize, too. "This doesn't happen often with Alexia," she says, to reassure us. "But every once in a while. . . . It was like this the night you arrived. I'm actually not *too* surprised. Family visits are wonderful, and they're an essential part of the treatment process, but sometimes they're overwhelming for the patient. I hope you won't take it personally, Camelia."

"Not at all," I say, knowing that it's far more than personal.

It's downright genetic.

## 13

*A*FTER THE INCIDENT at the facility, Mom and I head back to our B and B, where we sit in the dining room pushing the food around on our plates.

"I'm sorry," Mom says again, after what feels like an eternity of silence.

All during the car ride here, she just kept saying how she never would've agreed to let me spend time with Aunt Alexia—even to come on this trip—if she'd known how unstable my aunt really was.

"Ms. Connolly suggested that the outburst might be the result of hearing more voices," Mom says, feigning a bite of broccoli. "And all this time . . . I thought she was supposedly getting better."

"She *is* getting better," I insist, knowing how ridiculous the argument sounds.

Mom shakes her head. Her fork lands against her

plate with a clank. Meanwhile, my heart starts pounding, because I honestly don't know how to break it to her—that sometimes I hear voices, too.

"Maybe she doesn't belong at the facility," I venture.

"Of course she does." Mom sighs. "I see that more than ever now."

"No, I mean, maybe we should look into some other type of therapy—something a bit more forward-thinking or progressive."

"Ledgewood *is* forward-thinking. The doctors use all types of therapy in their practice—things like polarity, yoga, meditation. . . . Plus, you have to admit, it doesn't exactly have the feel of a regular mental hospital. The furnishings, the decor, the wide windows to let in plenty of natural light . . . Everything's been chosen with an eye toward health—"

"Well, it isn't working," I say, putting my fork down, too, "because staying there would make me sick." I look away, still able to picture the snail insignia, and too timid to tell her the truth—that maybe there's an alternative explanation as to why Aunt Alexia's hearing voices.

An explanation that no one's even considered.

The following morning, Mom and I pack up to leave, with plans to stop by Ledgewood en route to the airport. At first, Mom insists that I wait for her at the espresso bar down the road. She hands me a twenty and practically kicks me to the curb. But, after some major convincing on my part, she finally agrees to let me join her.

"I didn't come all this way to turn back now," I insist. "I wouldn't feel right about not saying good-bye."

Mom musters a smile, perhaps proud that I seem so concerned about Alexia. And I *am* concerned. But I also just want to see her again—to see if she has anything more to tell me, and to whisper in her ear that I know she isn't crazy.

Once inside the hospital, Mom is escorted to a meeting room, while I'm forced to wait in the lobby. There's a woman sitting across from me, probably in her late twenties. She looks perfectly normal, with normal clothes, and normal dark hair, and so I assume she must have family staying here, too. But then she starts eating a page from her magazine, ironically an ad for Snack Bits, and I know I've got her all wrong.

A moment later, Ms. Connolly calls the woman into another room, and not long after that, my mother reappears. She waves me over from the door that leads to what I'm guessing are the patients' rooms. I follow her down a long, narrow hallway to the room at the end.

While my mom stands guard at the door, I venture inside. Aunt Alexia's room looks much different from what I imagined. The walls are a deep shade of blue, her bed linens have a pretty violet pattern, and the lighting is soft rather than stark.

Aunt Alexia turns when she sees me. "I'm sorry about yesterday," she says, in a voice as tiny as she is. "Sometimes I get a little too wrapped up in my work."

"That happens," I say, almost wishing she could read my mind. "Is that more of your art?" I gesture toward some canvases piled up in the corner.

Aunt Alexia nods, and I go take a look, wishing that my mom would give us just a couple of moments alone. I sit on the edge of her bed, taking my time as I flip through paintings of all sorts, from the most disturbing image of a woman drowning in the ocean to an innocent portrait of a kitten sleeping with its mother.

I spend several minutes studying the images and searching for answers before I come across the portrait of Adam.

"You like that one, don't you?" she asks.

"It's just that he looks so familiar to me."

"You know this boy?"

I open my mouth, but no words come out. Meanwhile, another nurse comes to ensure that everything's okay. Mom exchanges a few words with him, but it's all in hushed tones, so I can't really hear.

Aunt Alexia checks to see that my mother is still pre-occupied and then pulls a painting from the middle of the pile. "Does this look familiar to you, too?" she asks.

It's a picture of a bloodstained knife. The handle of the knife is red and curls downward, perhaps for a better hold.

I stifle a gasp, covering my mouth and noticing how the tip of the knife is jagged, and how droplets of blood drip down toward the bottom of the canvas.

"You recognize it?" she asks.

I shake my head. "I've never seen a knife like that before."

"Not yet," she whispers. Her voice is just as cutting as the knife.

"Excuse me?"

"I couldn't get this image out of my mind the other night," she continues. "I did it right after the painting of the boy." She gestures to the picture of Adam. "And then I started hearing voices."

"What kind of voices?"

"Screaming," she says. "Like someone was about to die. And so I started screaming, too. That's when the nurses came."

I nod, trying to get a grip, almost tempted to look away, to excuse myself for just five solitary minutes.

But then: "Don't let him out of your sight," she hisses. She grasps my wrist. Her knuckles are taut and white.

"Excuse me?" I ask again.

"The boy with the snail insignia," she explains. "Don't let him out of your sight . . . or else he'll die."

A second later, I feel my mother grab me from behind. The male nurse comes to restrain my aunt, pinning her arms to her chest. But this time, Aunt Alexia doesn't fight back.

"I'm fine," I insist. "She didn't do anything wrong."

But the nurse doesn't listen, instead stabbing Alexia's thigh with a needle.

"Mom, stop him!" I shout.

The nurse rings a buzzer to page Ms. Connolly, and then tells us to leave right away.

"You're not crazy," I blurt out to Alexia. Tears fill my eyes.

But I'm not even sure she hears me. Aunt Alexia's body falls limp against her bed, her gaze no longer fiery, all the spirit inside her gone dead.

# AUDIO TRANSCRIPT 4

**DOCTOR:** You look happy today.

**PATIENT:** I am happy.

**DOCTOR:** Tell me about it.

**PATIENT:** *(Patient laughs.)*

**DOCTOR:** What's so funny?

**PATIENT:** *(Continues laughing.)*

**DOCTOR:** Do you need to take a moment outside to compose yourself?

**PATIENT:** No.

**DOCTOR:** Care to tell me then what you find so amusing?

**PATIENT:** That's for me to know and for you to find out.

**DOCTOR:** So now we're speaking in riddles?

**PATIENT:** He doesn't even know.


**DOCTOR:** Who doesn't?

**PATIENT:** *(More laughing.)*


**DOCTOR:** Could you stop laughing for a moment and tell me?

**PATIENT:** *(Laughing.)*


**DOCTOR:** You talked before about hurting yourself.

**PATIENT:** *Joked*, you mean.


**DOCTOR:** Okay, joked. Have you ever thought about hurting someone else?

**PATIENT:** Who hasn't?


**DOCTOR:** Are you thinking about it now?

**PATIENT:** Maybe. *(More laughing.)*


**DOCTOR:** Please stop laughing. Do we need to end this session early?

**PATIENT:** We can end it whenever you want.


**DOCTOR:** Why would you want to hurt someone?

**PATIENT:** Maybe the person deserves it. Maybe in some weird and twisted way, it's what he wants, too. That's why he behaves the way he does. He's like a child.

**DOCTOR:** Are you talking about your father?

**PATIENT:** God, no. That would be too easy.


**DOCTOR:** Then who?

**PATIENT:** Don't worry about it.


**DOCTOR:** I *am* worried.

**PATIENT:** I'm not going to do anything. They're only thoughts.


**DOCTOR:** Then why are you laughing?

**PATIENT:** Because my thoughts amuse me.

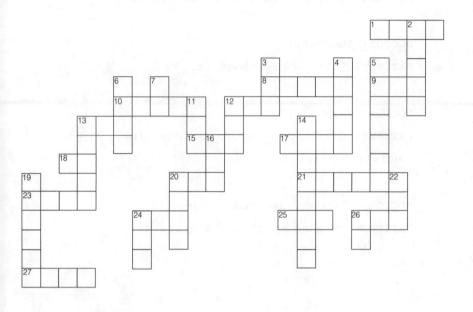

## Across

**1.** Covet.

**12.** Me + You = _____.

**24.** _____ are despicable.

## Down

**11.** Without _____ s, you will not see.

**13.** If I cut you, you will _____.

**22.** I _____ you in the daytime, and I watch you all night long.

14

ON THE FLIGHT BACK to Boston, I check my cell phone for messages, surprised to see that I have seven: four from Kimmie and two from Wes, both ranting at me for not giving them up-to-the-minute details about my trip.

The final message is from Ben. He doesn't really say much, just that he hopes that things are going well and he'll see me when I get home.

I flip my phone closed and glance at my mother. Her vacant stare is aimed down at her magazine, at an ad for hemorrhoid cream. She hasn't flipped a page in well over an hour. I want to talk to her about what could possibly be going on with Aunt Alexia and her powers, but I'm almost afraid she might actually believe that I'm going crazy, too.

Once we land and retrieve our bags, I head for the exit ramp, feeling completely anxious about the idea of getting back to my life. I mean, if it isn't overwhelming enough to have Adam's fate on my shoulders, I also feel like I need to fix things with my aunt.

Not that I'm complaining. It's just that I feel more responsible than I ever thought possible, and I'm not so sure I can handle it.

"Camelia?" Mom asks. "Are you feeling okay?"

It's the most she's said since we left Detroit, which obviously means that I must look pretty spooked.

"I'm fine," I lie, walking toward the arrivals area.

To my complete and utter shock, Ben is there, waiting for me. There's a bouquet of lilacs clenched in his hand.

Without a second thought, I drop my bag and rush into his arms.

"I guess this means that you didn't miss me at all," he jokes.

I bury my face into his coat, almost wishing he could swallow me whole.

Ben runs his fingers down the length of my back and then whispers in my ear: "Two days without you is definitely too much."

I look up into his face, hating the fact that we can't freeze this moment.

"I called you a couple of times on your cell, by the way," he says, "but I didn't want to explain things in a message. I really wanted to talk to you. I feel bad about the way we left things."

"We have a lot to talk about," I tell him.

"I know." The expression on his face is as grave as mine now.

"Camelia?" Mom calls from just behind me.

Subtly I try to wipe the buildup of emotion at the rims of my eyes. "Look who came to greet us," I tell her.

Mom gives him a quick hello. A second later, Dad emerges through the double doors and gives Mom a surprise attack hug. Mom can't help letting out a smile, but I can tell she's still distracted, even as Dad reveals what he's got in his pocket—a dairy-free brownie from Rawbert's, one of my Mom's favorite places to eat.

"I figured you'd be going through withdrawal by now," he jokes, referring to her lack of vegan cuisine over the weekend.

Mom gives him a tiny smooch on the cheek before turning to me. "I take it Ben will be driving you home."

"Is that okay?" I ask.

"It's fine," Dad says, answering for her. "But we'd better run. I'm double-parked."

While Ben and Dad load up the car, Mom gets into the front seat, seemingly eager to get away.

"Is she going to be okay?" Ben asks, once Dad drives off.

"Honestly? I don't know. Things got pretty ugly with my aunt. I'll fill you in on all the disturbing details later."

"And what about us?" he continues. "Are *we* going to be okay?"

"We have to be." I wipe my eyes again. "Because I'm not so sure I can make it through all of this without you."

"So you *need* me, is that it?" He grins.

I bite my lip, wishing I had the courage to tell him how I really feel.

That this is so far beyond need for me.

That it's beyond anything I've ever experienced before.

# 15

$\mathcal{I}$N MY ROOM, I tell Ben about what happened
with my aunt. And all the while, his expression
remains mostly unfazed, as if maybe he's known
the truth for some time now.

"I think Adam might really be in trouble," I insist.
"How else do you explain the portrait? My aunt doesn't
even know him. She's never even seen Adam before."

"As far you know, she doesn't know him."

"Seriously?" I raise an eyebrow.

"It's possible," he says, taking a seat at my desk. "I
mean, *you* met him. He sought you out, uprooted his life
to break into yours. Stranger things have happened."

"She would've mentioned it if she knew him."

"Maybe it wasn't even Adam in the painting. Maybe it
was just someone who looked like him."

"And maybe my horse sculpture was a coincidence,
too."

Ben takes my hand and pulls me close. "I'm only trying to be helpful."

"It was *him*," I say. "Aunt Alexia knew it, too. She knew the portrait had meaning to me. I mean, talk about strange things happening. It wasn't so long ago that the biggest drama in my life was what color to paint my pottery bowl."

"And now you have me in your life, and everything's completely—"

"Better."

"Yeah, right."

I squeeze his hand, hoping he can sense that I'm telling the truth. "A whole lot better."

"Minus the abductions, the psychotic gifts, and all the other stalker stuff."

"I want you in my life," I tell him.

"And you want this touch power of yours, too?"

"I don't think I have any other choice."

"I don't know." He grips my hand harder. "Maybe if I went away, it would go away, too."

"It didn't work that way the last time you left. And it didn't work that way for Aunt Alexia. There was no magical boy who came along one day and turned her power on. According to her journal, it wasn't until she was around my age that her power really started to develop."

"And now she's in a mental hospital because of it."

"Because she didn't know how to deal with it. She didn't know what it was, or why she was hearing voices. Her doctors didn't, either. They still don't. But it won't be that way with me."

"Are you sure?" he asks, perhaps feeling somehow responsible.

"Whatever's going on with my touch power has nothing to do with you. You didn't do this to me." I break his grip on my hand and run my fingers up the length of his arms, over his scar and then across his chest.

Ben draws me closer. My knees graze his inner thighs.

"So, let's just say for the sake of argument that Adam really *is* in trouble," he says. "What does the snail painting have to do with anything?"

"You think I know?"

"Why not?" He smiles. His fingers linger at the small of my back, beneath the hem of my sweater, sending tingles all over my skin. "You seem to have all the other answers."

I smile, too, flattered that he sees me that way, because I couldn't feel more confused.

The phone rings a second later, pulling the plug on what would otherwise be the beginning of a perfectly romantic make-up scene. I wait for my parents to answer, but they don't.

Mom and Dad have shut themselves up in their bedroom, no doubt also discussing the details of the trip.

"Hello?" I say, finally answering the phone on the sixth ring.

"Hey," Adam says. "How are you?"

Instead of responding, I lock eyes with Ben. Meanwhile, Adam chatters on about school and his apartment, about how his obnoxious roommate has finally moved out and how he'd love to get together some time.

"Sounds good," I say, knowing that we need to meet up soon.

Ben remains staring at me, clearly suspecting that it's Adam on the phone. After a few moments he gets up to put on his coat.

*Don't go*, I mouth to him.

"Camelia?" Adam says.

"Yeah," I mutter into the phone. "I'm still here."

"So, what do you say? Coffee? Dinner and a movie? Dinner and/or a movie? A movie and then coffee afterward—"

"Coffee," I say, cutting him off. "And it won't be a date."

"Of course not. This will just be a couple of old friends getting together over very civilized cups of java. We won't even request any froth."

"Okay," I agree, eager to get off the phone.

We make plans to meet tomorrow after school, and then I hang up.

Ben is waiting for me at the doorway.

"That was Adam," I say, as if he hadn't already figured it out.

"You didn't sound so surprised that he called."

"I wasn't surprised," I admit, proceeding to tell him that I'd called Adam after the incident in pottery class. "I just wanted to make sure that he was okay. I was really worried."

"Well, I'm worried, too." He looks away, making it

92

hard to decipher whether he's more angered or hurt.

"Worried because of Adam?"

"Because of a lot of things."

I cross the room to take his hand, hoping he can sense how open I'm being—how I no longer have anything to hide. "Come with me tomorrow when I meet with him. We'll work as a team."

"I don't know. I have a sneaking suspicion that Adam isn't expecting anyone to tag along, especially me."

"Who cares what he expects? We're talking about his life here."

"I know."

"Then what?"

"I just need some time alone." Still avoiding my gaze, he gives me a paltry peck on the cheek, and then heads out the door.

## 16

*I*T'S THREE A.M. I've been trying to fall asleep for the past four hours, but it obviously isn't working. Finally, I give up and head down to my studio in the basement. I wire off a slab of clay and wedge it out against my worktable, concentrating on the clammy texture and the way its familiarity soothes me. My eyes closed, a series of images runs across my mind. I let out a breath, trying to see which image actually sticks. And then I start to sculpt.

Using a rolling pin, I smooth the clay out until it's completely flat. Then I grab an X-Acto knife and cut out a bunch of square tiles, about an inch in length on all sides. I arrange the tiles against my work board, still focused on the image inside my head.

Pressed behind my eyes are squares that run both vertically and horizontally, intersecting one another to create a map of sorts. After a good hour or so, I have a whole slew of them. I place them against my board in a way that I feel makes sense.

In the end, I have something that resembles a crossword puzzle, minus the letters. I sit back on my stool and study its shape—at the top right the tiles form a capital $T$; in the bottom left, they make the shape of a capital $L$. There are numerous tiles positioned in the middle—a section of which almost looks like stairs—but I'm not quite sure I've placed everything right.

I cover it all over with a tarp and then return to my room, my mind more relaxed despite the surge of new questions. Still, I'm hopeful I'll fall asleep.

Before homeroom at school the next day, Ben pulls up beside me in the parking lot on his motorcycle. He cuts his engine and removes his helmet. "Are you still meeting Adam today?" he asks.

"Definitely," I tell him. "And I'd definitely like your help. I mean, I know this is really hard for you—"

"But you're worth it." He reaches out to touch the side of my face. The heat of his hand penetrates my whole body. "I'll do whatever I can."

"Then be honest with me." I take his hand and kiss his palm. "Unlike *some* people, I can't read minds. And I know there's a lot you're not telling me."

Ben nods, but still he doesn't come clean.

"Did you change your mind about coming with me after school?" I continue.

His dark gray eyes search my face, as if he were

seriously considering the question. "I really think Adam will be less on guard if it's just the two of you. You'll be able to find out more. Plus, what am I supposed to do?" He smirks. "Ask him to hold my hand?"

"No." I smirk back. "But you could touch his keys or something."

"You can do this," he insists. "And I'll be here for you when you get back." Ben steps off his bike and reaches out to take my books. As he does so, I notice some writing scrawled across the cover of one of his notebooks: the words *WATCH YOUR BACK,* in black capital letters.

"What's that?" I ask, pointing to the message. There's a twisting sensation inside my gut.

Ben hesitates, as if fully aware that I'm thoroughly freaked. "It's something I scribbled down late last night, after I left your house . . . when I couldn't fall asleep. Those words just wouldn't get out of my head, and so I wrote them down in case they were relevant."

"They wouldn't get out of your head?"

"Sort of like what happened to you in pottery class," he says. "Maybe you're rubbing off on me more than you know."

"I don't understand," I say, touching my head where there's now a dull ache.

"The phrase popped into my head as soon as I touched you yesterday," he explains. "At the airport. I assumed it was a message for me—that maybe I needed to watch *my* back—but then I remembered your aunt's outburst. Were there any other choice phrases she happened to mention during your trip?"

"Not that I can remember."

"So, maybe it's just the result of my needing more than four hours of sleep at night." He wedges the notebook between a couple of books, so no one can see it. "All I need is for someone to accuse me of walking around flashing harassing messages."

I'm tempted to ask more about the message—to see if, once again, he's being intentionally cryptic—but it's already 8:11, and he's saved by the proverbial bell. At least for now.

# 17

$\mathcal{I}$T'S AFTER SCHOOL, and Kimmie, Wes, and I are sitting in Wes's car outside the sandwich shop where Adam's insisted I meet him.

"I thought he said coffee," Kimmie says, peeking out at the shop's logo of a rat eating a meatball sub.

"He did, but apparently this place has really great food."

"Or so the rats think," she says, lowering her cat's-eye sunglasses to get a better look at the place.

Wes squirts two jets of breath freshener onto his tongue, the peppermint smell of which reminds me of an old lady's purse. "Are you planning to tell him about all your funky touch stuff?" he asks, followed by a couple of obnoxious exhalations.

I shake my head and lean back to avoid the peppermint fumes. "Nor am I going to tell him about how my aunt painted his portrait."

"Not ready to come out of the touch-and-tell closet,

eh?" He points to the heart-shaped decal on his dashboard, the center of which reads: LOVE IS THE ANSWER. GIVE DIVERSITY A CHANCE.

"It's not like he'd believe all this touchy stuff anyway," Kimmie says. "And who *would*? Does Adam even know about Ben's powers?"

"No," I remind her. "No one really knows about that except us. And let's keep it that way."

"So, then, how are you going to convince him that his ass is grass, that his dude is dead, that his crust is dust?" Wes asks.

"I'm just going to fish around," I tell them. "I'll take mental notes, ask lots of questions, and see if anything seems off."

"Sounds like a stellar time to me," he says mockingly. "I'm sure Adam will be thrilled."

"This isn't about stellar times," I say. "It's about making sure that he's okay—that nothing bad is going to happen to him."

"I repeat," Wes yawns, "I'm sure it'll be stellar."

I ignore him and open the car door. Wes waits until I enter the shop before pulling away from the curb.

Adam is already inside.

"Hey," he says, standing up from one of the back tables.

He looks good—even better than I remembered. His wavy brown hair is a bit shaggier than the last time I saw him, and his shoulders seem broader, too.

I make my way toward him, noticing how small the

place is inside, set up sort of bistro-style, with checked tablecloths and cityscape posters on the walls. A giant chalkboard menu hangs behind the counter, and cooks prepare the food in full view of the customers.

"Hungry?" Adam asks, gesturing for me to sit.

At the same moment, one of the cooks rings a bell for what turns out to be Adam's order—a brimming bowl of curly fries with tartar sauce on the side. "I took the liberty of ordering us some hors d'oeuvres," he jokes. "But you're welcome to get whatever else you like."

"This looks perfect," I say, peeling off my coat.

Adam sets me up with a plate and napkin, and then starts gabbing away about how he and his study buddies come here at least every other night.

"So, you've made a lot of friends at school?" I ask, eager to steer the conversation into more personal territory.

We end up talking about how his semester's going, how he's taking an Intro to Drafting class, and how he's thrilled to have an apartment of his own.

"At first I thought I wouldn't be able to afford it," he says. "But I got a really good job at an art-supply store down the road. I get a discount on drafting tools, and they pay me time and a half on the weekends and holidays."

"That's great," I say.

"It's actually better than great, because I've already met a couple of architects in the area. With some good old-fashioned schmoozing, I'm hoping to be able to work my way into one of the firms, maybe as an intern."

I nod, genuinely happy for him, because I know this is

what he really wants, and I've seen how truly talented he is. About a month ago, he crafted me a model of Camelia's House of Clay, the pottery shop I might own one day, even adding in tiny wooden tables, and shelves full of greenware.

"And how's Ben doing?" he segues. "Are you two still seeing each other?"

"Do you really want to be talking about this?" I ask, for the sake of his feelings.

He pauses midchew. His dark brown eyes scrunch up in confusion. "Why not? Unless I'm touching on a sore spot?"

"No sore spots. Things between Ben and me are good."

"Then how come you don't sound so sure?" He grins.

"I *am* sure," I say, but I don't think he hears me. There's a girl standing at our table now. She's pretty, with bobbed dark hair and eyes the color of pale blue sea glass.

"Who's your friend?" she asks Adam, before either of us has a chance to say hello.

"Camelia, this is my friend Piper," Adam says, by way of introduction.

A couple of girls stand slightly behind her. "And that's Melissa and Janet," he continues.

"Make that Jungle Girl Janet," Piper says, "who just won her fourth competition for her talent on the trapeze."

"Piper's sort of my biggest fan." Janet blushes.

"Well, congratulations," I tell her.

"Thanks." She smiles, tugging nervously on her braid. "Do you go to Hayden, too?"

"Actually, I'm still in high school," I confess.

"My sympathies to you," Piper says. "I would absolutely *die* if I had to go back to raising my hand just to get up out of my seat, or answering to a school bell."

"Not to mention immature boys, the humiliation they call gym class, and tons of pointless homework." Melissa brings a strand of her strawberry blond hair up to her mouth for a chew.

"Okay, so minus the gym class, college actually isn't so much *unlike* high school," Piper jokes. "So, are we still on for tonight?" she asks Adam, taking a sip of his root beer.

"Or will you be spending the rest of your day hanging out with high school girls?" Melissa mooches a curly fry from our plate. She dips it into the tartar sauce and then shoves it between her freckled lips.

Adam ignores her comment, proceeding to tell me that he and Piper are working on a project together for school.

"Not just *any* project," she insists. "We've been assigned to be husband and wife in accounting class. We have to work out all our bills on his football coach's salary. I'm a stay-at-home mom with four kids, three dogs, and a parakeet. Is that supercute, or what?"

"More like super high school," Melissa says before I can answer. "I think I did a similar assignment in health class."

"Well, whatever," Piper says, swatting the negative words away. There are frowny faces painted on her candy pink fingernails. "I need an A, and Professor Williams hates me, which means I have to be twice as economical with all my debits and three times as stingy with all my credits. So, I'll see you at eight?" she asks Adam.

"Sounds good," he says.

While Piper and her friends head for the exit, Adam leans in close and apologizes for Melissa. "She can be a bit prickly at times."

"Well, Piper seems nice."

"A little too nice, actually. She's one of those girls who gets walked on a lot."

"But not by you. I mean, you two are just friends, right?"

"Right." He grins, perhaps misreading my interest. "Friends. Just like you and me."

I clear my throat, suddenly realizing how little I've accomplished during this conversation. "So, everything with you is great?" I say in a final attempt to get some scoop. "No problems? No demons in your closet? Nothing weird going on?"

"Other than this conversation? What's up with you?" he asks, double-dipping a fry. "You were like this on the phone the other day, too."

"Just making conversation."

"Psycho conversation, maybe."

"Speaking of psychos," I half joke, "any in your life that I should know about?"

"Just one," he says, giving me a pointed look.

"Very funny," I say, wondering if maybe I *am* being psycho—if maybe this whole scene was just a really bad idea.

We sit in awkward silence for several seconds, picking at the shrinking mound of curly fries, and sipping our drinks down to the ice. But then Adam slips his parka on, complaining of a chill.

And that's when I see it.

The small insignia on his jacket, right by the collar. It's a diamond-shaped logo with a snail inside.

Exactly like what Aunt Alexia and I painted.

"I mean, seriously," Adam says, "is it really so hard to believe that for the first time in a long time I'm really happy with the way my life is going?" He continues to jabber on, but I'm not really paying attention.

My pulse races and my mouth goes dry.

"Camelia?" he asks.

I force myself to look into his face.

"So, is it?" he asks.

"Is what?" I gaze at the scar on his bottom lip, reminded of my sculpture in pottery class.

"Is it so hard to believe that I'm happy?" he asks. "That everything is going great with me, for once?"

"No," I lie, at a complete loss for something better to say. "It isn't so hard to believe at all."

# AUDIO TRANSCRIPT 5

**DOCTOR:** I'd like to focus our session today on riddles.

**PATIENT:** You mean, jokes?

**DOCTOR:** More like puzzles, questions, things that don't readily have an answer.

**PATIENT:** Why would you want to talk about that?

**DOCTOR:** Because I think you like riddles. I get the sense that you enjoy it when I don't know all the answers.

**PATIENT:** If you can't figure things out, then maybe you shouldn't be a therapist.

**DOCTOR:** Seems like I've struck a chord.

**PATIENT:** *(Patient doesn't respond.)*

**DOCTOR:** You talked last time about wanting to hurt someone. You said this person was a male, and that deep down, he might in fact want to be hurt.

**PATIENT:** You read too much into things.

**DOCTOR:** It's what you said. I can play it back for you if you'd like.

**PATIENT:** No, thanks.

**DOCTOR:** Are you still thinking about hurting this person?

**PATIENT:** Like I said, you read too much into things.

**DOCTOR:** Do I? Or is this all part of one big game?

**PATIENT:** Let's just say that someone is making a big mistake and I'm doing my best to protect that person.

**DOCTOR:** By hurting someone else?

**PATIENT:** I didn't say that.

**DOCTOR:** Then why don't you explain it?

**PATIENT:** *(Patient laughs.)*

**DOCTOR:** What's so funny?

**PATIENT:** Maybe you're right. Maybe I do like puzzles. Maybe I like them a whole lot.

**DOCTOR:** And why is that funny?

**PATIENT:** Because with every game, there can only be one winner.

**DOCTOR:** Sometimes there's a tie.

**PATIENT:** That's what sudden death is for.

**DOCTOR:** Whose sudden death?

**PATIENT:** It's an expression.

**DOCTOR:** Is it?

**PATIENT:** *(No response.)*

**DOCTOR:** Would you ever consider forfeiting a game?

**PATIENT:** I'm not a quitter.

**DOCTOR:** It wouldn't be considered quitting if you'd learned something, if you no longer *needed* to play and wanted to move on.

**PATIENT:** But I do need to play. I need to win.

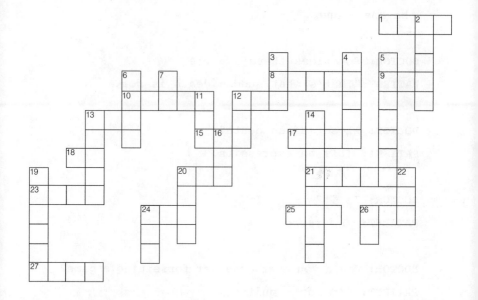

## Across

**25.** Opposite of live.

## Down

**5.** To be entitled to.

**7.** When you make a mistake, you need

_____ pay the consequences.

**24.** Opposite of me.

*A*FTER OUR MEETING at the sandwich shop, Adam offers me a ride home, and I know I should probably take it. I know it will probably give me more of an opportunity to pry deeper into his life.

But I really need to get away.

And so I take off down the street, in the opposite direction of where he's headed, and duck into a bookshop. I pull out my cell phone and dial Kimmie's number.

"Where are you?" she asks. "Wes and I'll come pick you up."

I give her the address, and they're here in less than the time it takes me to read through the first chapter of *Spy Girl*.

"Well?" Kimmie asks, joining me in the backseat.

I give her the lowdown, and she lays right into me: "I cannot believe you let Adam off so easily."

"I know." I sigh. "I feel like such a failure."

"Or maybe you're just paranoid," Wes says. "I mean, have you considered that maybe you're wrong about him?"

"I'm not willing to take that chance. Too much has happened. There are way too many red flags to call what's been going on a coincidence."

"My vote? You suck at subtlety," Kimmie says, obviously referring to my prying skills. "But, lucky for you, I don't suck."

"At subtlety, that is." Wes smirks.

Kimmie middle-finger-scratches her nose at him. "Where does Adam live? We'll go by his place, and I'll help you get some answers."

"I don't know." I shrug.

"Seriously?" She evil-eyes me. "You dated the guy."

"It wasn't exactly dating."

"Which is still no excuse. Call the boy. Get his address. And I'll do all the talking."

I take out my cell phone and rest it on my lap. "And what do you suggest I give as an excuse for needing to drop by his place?"

"Booty call?" Wes suggests.

"Blame it on me," Kimmie says, fishing out an eyeliner pencil from her Tupperware-container purse. "Tell him that we were in the area, picking you up, that we got talking about schools, and I mentioned being interested in his. It wouldn't be completely unheard-of if I wanted to check out my housing options."

"He'll see right through it," I tell her.

"Not that it matters," she says. "I mean, the boy is totally hot for you, right?"

"I'd put him more in the warm category."

"So he'll want to see you regardless of your lame-o excuse."

"Yes, but he'll think I'm interested."

"Look, do you want to figure this all out or not?" she asks, applying a thick ring of purple around one eye.

"I do," I tell her. And so, I flip my phone open and dial his number.

## 19

AS KIMMIE PREDICTED, Adam doesn't question the excuse. I'm not even sure he hears it. Because, no sooner do I mutter the words "Do you think we could stop by?" than he's giving me directions, landmarks, and alternate routes.

We pull up in front of his apartment building. It's tall, brick, and dingy-looking, sandwiched between a feline hospital and a place called Busty's Bar. We enter a dank lobby, and are confronted by a set of elevators. A giant OUT OF ORDER sign is tacked across the doors.

"Lovely," Wes says, nodding toward a puddle on the floor. Buckets have been set up in a lame attempt to catch the dripping water that must trickle down from the broken-tiled ceiling during rainstorms.

"It smells like moldy Cheez Whiz," Kimmie says, scrunching up her nose.

I look around for a security buzzer, figuring that

Adam will have to buzz us up, but it seems there's no security whatsoever.

"Are you sure you got the address right?" Kimmie asks. "I wouldn't even let my dad's new girlfriend stay here. Did I happen to mention he's dating a child?"

"Now, now," Wes says, giving her shoulder a good patting. "Nineteen years old is hardly a child. She's old enough to sign a contract, buy porn and cigarettes, and cross state lines with your dad if she wants to."

"Unfortunately, I think you just summed up their Saturday night," she says.

"We definitely need to talk about this later," I insist, giving her a hug.

We climb two flights up the emergency stairs to Adam's apartment. The door is already open.

"Hey!" Adam says, peeking into the hallway, clearly having been anticipating our arrival.

"We're here to scope out your place," Kimmie says, pushing past him into the apartment. We enter the kitchen. It's separated from the living room by just a couple of support beams, making the two rooms feel like one.

The girls from the sandwich shop are there, as well as Tray, Adam's friend from school.

"Hey," Tray says, nodding in my direction. His hair is long, dark, and straight, pulled back in a low ponytail, exactly like Jungle Girl Janet's. The two of them are sitting together, watching a gymnastics competition on Adam's big TV screen.

Meanwhile, Melissa and Piper completely ignore us—

they're too busy hovering over what appears to be an old yearbook at the kitchen island. Piper lets out a peal of laughter, and Melissa giggles along with her.

"Seriously," Piper says to Adam, "what were you thinking by wearing Hawaiian shorts and work boots to the prom?"

"Who cares?" Melissa says. "He still looks hot. I mean, check out those sexy legs."

"More like pigeon legs," Tray calls out.

The girls ignore the remark and continue to paw at his picture. And, honestly, if I didn't know better, I'd say Adam had his very own fan club.

"Adam tells us you guys are thinking about coming to Hayden," Melissa says, finally acknowledging our arrival. "Is that true?"

"It's true for me," Kimmie says.

Melissa eyes Kimmie's lace-and-latex skirt. "Well, just so you know, it's a whole lot harder to get in here than one might think. They don't just accept *anyone*."

"I think I can handle it," Kimmie says, completely on to her bitchery. "I've been able to sign my name and write a check since the third grade."

"Do you all live in the building?" I ask, in an effort to change the subject.

"Everyone but me." Piper frowns. She moves into the living room and plunks herself down on Tray's lap. "I still live at home with my overprotective parents, but I'd give anything to have my own place."

"Well, I must admit, I'm less than impressed,"

Kimmie says, staring at a crack in the wall. "I mean, no parking garage, no doorman out front . . ."

"No security cameras," Wes adds, pointing back toward the hallway.

"Well, you know, this isn't actual student housing," Adam says.

"Right." Melissa snickers. "I doubt the school would be able to afford liability insurance for a hole like this."

"And how's the neighborhood?" Kimmie persists. "Would I feel secure walking around the streets at night?"

"Funny," Melissa says folding her arms across her chest, "but Adam didn't mention that you were a street-walker. Is that how you'll be paying for school?"

"Why, are you looking for extra work?" Kimmie asks.

"Don't mind Melissa," Piper says. "She just failed a history test and got bitched out by her mom."

"Plus, we should probably go," Janet says.

"Finally." Tray practically pushes Piper off him. He gets up and makes a beeline for the door.

Piper reminds Adam once again about their study session later, and then, within sixty seconds, all of them are gone.

"Well, that was about as pleasant as having my ass waxed," Wes says.

"Sorry about Melissa," Adam says. "We went on a date last week, and things have been awkward ever since."

"Awkward meaning you two-timed her and got caught?" Wes asks. "Or meaning she gave off a sisterly vibe, and, as a result, you're still trying to shake it and/or her."

"I'd go with the latter," Kimmie says, ever the clinician. "Because she's obviously still too into you for the pure, unfettered hatred that could result from option number one."

"Not bad," Adam says, seemingly impressed. "But not quite accurate, either. Just after our date, I found out that Tray had a thing for her, too. And so I started giving Melissa the cold shoulder. Not the most mature way to break things off, but what can I say?"

"You're a guy," Kimmie sighs. "Say no more."

"So, I take it Melissa doesn't have a thing for Tray?" I ask.

"No, but Janet does. Of course, he's not interested in her." Adam shakes his head. "It's all so bogus and complicated. You think you're done with drama in high school, but it's just as bad in college."

"And, speaking of college," Kimmie gives Adam's arm a tug, "care to take me on that tour? How else am I going to know whether or not to apply?"

While Kimmie continues to deploy her prying skills, Adam leads her down a short hallway to where I assume the bedrooms are, and Wes moves into the living room to rifle through the stack of Adam's mail on the coffee table.

"Just leave it," I say, scolding him.

Wes ignores me, pulling forth what appears to be a crossword puzzle. "What's this?" he asks.

I take a closer look, noting the shape of the puzzle—the way the tiles form a capital $T$ in the far right corner, and a capital $L$ in the lower left. There's a sea of tiles between the two letter shapes.

Exactly like what I sculpted last night.

"What's wrong?" Wes asks, noticing my alarm.

Before I can answer, Adam returns to the kitchen, having finished playing tour guide. Luckily, however, thanks to Kimmie, they remain at the kitchen island, with their backs toward us.

"So, would you say that most everyone in the building is pretty normal?" Kimmie asks, still fishing for information. "There's no one I'd need to worry about? Because my parents are pretty anal about that sort of thing," she lies. "I swear, if it were up to them, I'd probably be living at home for the rest of my life."

Adam tries to address her concerns as best he can. Meanwhile, I grab a pen and get to work on the puzzle, noticing that there are only three questions, even though the puzzle's big—with enough tiles to fit over twenty different answers. Still, I solve the riddles fairly quickly; the answers are all pretty obvious.

"I just don't get it," I whisper, knowing there must be some significance here. I mean, what kind of crossword puzzle only gives you a few of the questions and leaves the remainder of the puzzle unsolved? And, since when are those questions so easy? So foolproof?

"What's wrong?" Wes says again. "Do you need to be medicated? Because I only brought my Pez along with me today." He flashes me his SpongeBob dispenser.

"Watch your back," I whisper, reading the crossword puzzle answers aloud.

"Okay, fine," Wes snaps, taking his Pez offering back. "But a simple 'no thank you' would have sufficed."

"You don't understand," I snap, holding the crossword puzzle out to him. *"WATCH YOUR BACK."*

Wes tilts his head, trying to make sense of what I mean. "I guess, if you really read into it, but it could also be *BACK WATCH YOUR,* or *YOUR BACK WATCH.* Not to mention that there's a huge hunk of the puzzle undone."

I shake my head and tell him that Ben had written the same message across the cover of his notebook—that he'd sensed the phrase and couldn't get it out of his head.

"What are you guys looking at?" Adam asks, standing just behind us now. He glances in the direction of his stack of mail, nearly half of which is already ransacked. But before he can squawk about it, I hold the crossword up to him.

"Where did you get this?" I ask.

"I don't know." He shrugs. "I get tons of junk from the student activities office."

A second later, Adam's cell phone rings. He picks it up. *It's Piper,* he mouths to us. "Yes, I'll be there," he tells her.

While he continues his phone call in private, Kimmie snatches the crossword puzzle out of my hands. She takes a moment to look it over before glaring straight back at me. "Watch your back," she whispers.

"Exactly," I say.

"Let the games begin," Wes sings. He pulls back the head of his Pez dispenser and downs the entire contents.

# 20

THE CROSSWORD PUZZLE is still clenched in Kimmie's grip; I take it back, hoping that Ben might be able to sense something from it.

"Can someone please tell me what's going on?" Adam asks, finally flipping his phone shut.

I hold the puzzle out to him again. "You don't think this looks off?"

"Not really," he says, barely giving it a second look.

"Someone thinks you should watch your back."

"No," he says. "Someone thinks I have time to waste on crossword puzzles."

"There's more to it," I insist.

"Why are you going through my mail?" he asks Wes.

"He wasn't going through it," I lie. "I saw the puzzle and filled it in."

"And now you think someone's out to get me?"

"I just think it's weird," I say, for lack of a better explanation.

"This whole scene is weird." He looks at Kimmie and then back at me.

Part of me wants to tell him about my sculptures. Another part isn't ready to expose what I know or how I know it.

"You haven't received any other puzzles like this, have you?" I ask, thinking about the series of stalker photos I received last fall.

"Actually . . ." Adam grabs the garbage pail by his desk and starts to pick through the trash. He pulls out a ball of crumpled paper and tosses it to me.

I smooth it out against my stomach.

It's another crossword puzzle, with the exact same shape as the one I just filled out, only there are different clues at the bottom.

"I got that one yesterday," he says.

"And the other one today?" I ask.

He nods. "I think student activities must have some kind of game going on. They're always sending out stuff like this. For the fall, it was a scavenger hunt, so that people could get used to the campus. Then, just before the holidays, they sent these paper-mitten cutout things, so that people would remember to donate."

"Have any of your friends received crossword puzzles?"

"I don't know." He shrugs. "We don't normally discuss our junk mail."

"Could you ask them anyway?"

"First, tell me what's going on."

I focus on the crumpled puzzle for a moment. I'm able to crack a couple of the clues right away: the words *always* and *watching*.

"You can call her a paranoid schizo all you want," Kimmie says.

"God knows I do," Wes mumbles.

"But the fact of the matter is that Camelia's been through a lot," she continues. "And so she likes to play it safe, especially when it comes to her friends."

"Look, I appreciate your concern," Adam says. "I really do. But—"

"But nothing," I say, interrupting him. I stuff both crossword puzzles into my pocket and tell Kimmie and Wes it's time to go.

# 21

*O*N THE RIDE BACK HOME, I grab a pen and resume the puzzle that Adam fished from the trash. It doesn't take me long to finish it. Once again, the clues are pretty simple to solve. I write the answers in one straight line and work to unscramble the message.

"What's the verdict?" Kimmie asks, peering back at me.

I stare down at the jumble of words. "I can't quite tell yet."

"Give us a clue," Wes says. "I love puzzles."

"That's because you are one," Kimmie jokes.

I read them the list of words: ARE, ALONE, YOU, NEVER, EYE, WATCHING, ALWAYS, AM.

Not five seconds later, Wes has the whole thing figured out: "YOU ARE NEVER ALONE. EYE AM ALWAYS WATCHING!" he says, making his voice all deep and throaty.

"Wait, seriously?" I ask, completely bewildered by the idea that he'd be able to unravel the message so quickly. I look at the individual words, making sure they're all included, and that he didn't add any extra.

"What can I say? I'm good at puzzles."

"Are you good at *making* them, too?" Kimmie asks. "Because it's a little scary how you were able to figure that out so fast."

"Do you think it matters that the 'eye' in the puzzle is the noun and not the pronoun?" I ask them.

"Since when is it a requirement for psychos to be good in English?" Wes asks.

"Only *you* would know." Kimmie glares at him.

"Plus, it's a puzzle," he says, ignoring her comment. "You have to expect a few quirks."

"I don't know," I say, still staring at the words. "Maybe there's some other message here. Maybe we need to try unscrambling it another way."

"Such as 'EYE AM NEVER ALONE. YOU ARE ALWAYS WATCHING,'" he suggests. "Or perhaps the ever-favorite 'YOU ARE NEVER WATCHING. EYE AM ALWAYS ALONE.'"

Kimmie scoots farther away from him in her seat. "Okay, you really *are* starting to scare me."

"I'm pretty sure you had it right the first time," I say, flipping to the WATCH YOUR BACK puzzle and thinking how Ben had predicted the words.

I take a moment to study the paper the crosswords were done on. They're bright white and of ample weight, making it clear the puzzles aren't photocopies. I hold them up to my nose, curious to see if I can detect any scent.

"Um, what are you doing?" Wes asks, looking at me through his rearview mirror.

"They smell like candy," I say.

"Well, they *were* in the garbage," he points out. "At least, one of them was, and I could've sworn I spotted a Mr. Goodbar wrapper in there."

"Why do you think this person would only give us a few of the puzzle clues?" I ask.

"Because they obviously want to string us along," Wes says. "Feed us messages whenever they feel like it . . . keep us playing this stupid game."

"You need to talk to Adam," Kimmie says. "You need to tell him to take this seriously."

"I agree," I say, shoving the puzzles back into my pocket. But first I need to talk to Ben.

As soon as Wes drops me off at home, I head up to my room to give Ben a call. He picks up right away, and I fill him in on what happened. "So, can you come over?" I ask, plopping down onto my bed. "I'd really like for you to try and sense something from the puzzles."

"You know my senses aren't always reliable with objects," he says. "Plus, the crosswords have been in your pocket all this time. I'll probably just sense you."

"You could still give it a try," I say, surprised at his hesitation.

It's quiet on the line for several seconds, as if he's trying to decide. "Can I call you later?" he asks. "My aunt wants me to have a look at the engine of her car."

"I thought you were going to help me," I say. "I thought we were a team."

"I am. We *are*."

"Then what's with the brush-off?"

"It's not a brush-off. I just have to go. Can I call you later?" he asks again.

"Don't worry about it," I say. My heart suddenly feels heavy. I tell him I'm going to bed, and then wish him a good night before hanging up. The phone clenched firmly against my chest, it rings just moments after we disconnect. "Having second thoughts?" I say.

"How did you know?" Adam asks.

"Oh, sorry." I press my eyes shut. "I guess I was kind of expecting someone else."

"Someone like Ben?"

"I'm glad you called," I say, ignoring the question.

"Yeah," he says. "Me, too. You kind of got me thinking, aka paranoid, and so I sifted through some of the piles of papers and stuff on my desk. I knew I'd gotten some more of those puzzles in the mail."

"And?"

"I was right. I found two more."

"Did you try to solve them?"

"That's kind of what I wanted to talk to you about, but I think we should discuss it in person. I could come by and pick you up. We could go and grab a coffee or something."

"No," I demand. "Tell me now."

"Well, the first puzzle I filled in didn't really bother me too much," he says. "It just said, 'YOU LIED TO ME.'"

"And the second?" I ask, standing up, somehow already suspecting the answer.

"It said that I deserved to die."

# 22

I TELL MY PARENTS that Adam's picking me up and that we're going to the Hayden College library to study together. Dad couldn't be happier with the news. Once the star forward on his high school and college soccer teams, Dad has adored Adam—or at least, Adam's former high school soccer stardom—ever since he first met him.

I grab my books and head out the door just as Adam's '70s Ford Bronco pulls in to the driveway, triggering the overhead sensor light. Ever since what happened last fall, my dad has made a feeble though still earnest attempt at safeguarding our place. He's put stickers on all the windows and poked yard signs into the lawn, both of which claim that we have a security system (we don't). He's also installed motion-detector lights that go on and off pretty much whenever they feel like it.

"Thanks for coming out," Adam says before opening

the passenger-side door for me.

I climb inside. The interior smells like peppermint stick. "What about your meeting tonight with Piper?" I ask, suddenly remembering their marriage assignment.

"I think this is more important."

I nod, noticing how good he looks in dark-washed jeans and a chest-hugging sweater.

It's just the kind of thing Kimmie warned me about: "He's totally going to get the wrong idea," she said of our impromptu meeting tonight. I'd called her as soon as I got off the phone with him, as soon as I'd agreed to let him pick me up. "You know he's going to use this as an opportunity to try and get back together with you."

"I'm just trying to help him," I told her. "I have no intention of anything shady."

"Yes, but things happen, Ms. Chameleon. People are weak. Plus, how come you never mentioned how hot Adam is? I mean, honestly, that boy's a scorcher."

"This isn't a date."

"Oh, *no?* Have you told Ben that you're going?"

"Ben's too busy to care."

"Would he care if Adam were lying to you about finding more crossword puzzles?"

"Um, what are you talking about?"

"Ever think this might be Adam's way of bonding with you?" she asked. "Maybe he saw how concerned you were about him and thought pretending to have more puzzles was the ticket to getting your attention."

"I don't think that's it."

"But it's possible," she said, reminding me how Adam tricked me once before. "It's also possible that—say, for the sake of argument, he *did* indeed find more puzzles— he's merely faking his concern over them."

"Seriously?" I asked, ever-awed by her corrupt and suspicious mind.

"Seriously *possible*," she insisted.

Still, suspicious mind or not, by the end of our conversation, Kimmie finally agreed that it was a good idea I was going to meet him.

"So, where do you want to go?" Adam asks, turning to face me. His deep brown eyes match the color of his sweater.

"The library," I say, assuming I'll feel a tinge less guilty if we actually go along with the story I told my parents.

Adam doesn't question the choice. He simply puts his car in drive and we arrive about fifteen minutes later.

The library is surprisingly full. Adam leads us through the stacks, mentioning how there are study rooms in the back where we can talk in private. He nods toward an open door, but before we even get there, someone calls out his name.

We turn to look. It's Piper. She, Melissa, Janet, and Tray are sitting around a table, doing their homework. Janet waves, while Melissa shoots us a dirty look and Tray stays focused on his books, ignoring our existence.

"Busted," Piper says, once we get to their table. Her arms are folded; she's clearly ticked. "I thought you said you were too busy to work on our project."

"I am. I *did*," he says, flustered. "It's sort of a long story."

"One that obviously involves minors." Melissa snickers. "Isn't it past your bedtime, little girl?"

"Don't be like that," Adam says to her.

"Like what?" she snaps. "Don't be a scammer like you? Don't stand people up? Don't lead people on?"

"I thought we were all going to move past this," Adam says.

Melissa gets up and stomps off. Meanwhile, Tray has yet to even look up from his book.

"We'll talk later, okay?" Adam says to Piper.

"How about I come by your place and show you what I've done on the project?" she says. "I could bring over some late-night snacks. . . ."

"Sounds good," he says. We head into a study room and shut the door behind us.

"*That* was intense," I say, my back pressed against the door.

"No," he argues. "*This* is intense." He pulls a couple of folded pieces of paper from his jacket pocket and tosses them onto the table.

I take one, noting the familiar creamy texture of the paper, and the same sweet scent. Before I can open it up, there's a knock on the door. Adam goes to answer it.

Melissa is there. "This study room is actually taken," she says, shoving a sheet of paper in his face—what I'm assuming is a reservation form.

"Since when?" Adam asks. "We just got here."

"Since about two minutes ago." She points out the time on the sheet. "I just reserved it. Go complain at the circulation desk." She pushes past us into the room and begins spreading all her things out on the table.

"Let's go," Adam says. He hands me the other crossword puzzle, and we leave, ending up back in his Bronco.

"I'm sorry," he says, smacking the steering wheel. "I honestly don't know what's wrong with everybody."

"You pissed them off. It's not exactly rocket science."

"I didn't know Tray was interested in her. He could've said something. Plus, I broke things off as soon as I found out."

"And now Melissa's bitter because of it."

"Whatever," he says, staring up at the ceiling.

I pull the crossword puzzles out of my pocket. They look exactly like the others, with the *T*-shape in the far right corner and the *L*-shape at the lower left.

"Pretty freaky, huh?" he asks.

"To say the least."

"So, I think you have some explaining to do."

"Excuse me?"

"Come on, Camelia." He turns toward me. "Ever since you called me, you've been hinting that something's not right. It's like you know something. So, what is it? Is it something you heard? Is it part of some game?"

I glance out the window, wondering what to tell him—what I can say that he'll actually believe. "Let's go someplace to talk."

"You name it."

Still parked in front of the library, I continue to look out the window, searching for a coffee shop or restaurant—someplace casual where we can go to discuss things. But it appears as if most of the surrounding buildings belong to the college.

"I know at least one place that's private," he says, starting the ignition. He pulls away from the curb, and in less than two minutes we're in front of his apartment building. "Is this okay?"

"I guess," I say, hoping I'm not making a mistake. My cell phone clutched in my hand, I enter the lobby with him, and we move up the stairs. There's a tightening sensation inside my chest.

Adam swings open the door to his floor, and we start down the hallway to his apartment. But then I feel myself come to a sudden halt.

My hand flies over my mouth.

"What's wrong?" he asks, before he actually sees it.

On his door.

In bright red letters.

The words *YOU DESERVE TO DIE* scream inside my head and nearly knock me to the ground.

# AUDIO TRANSCRIPT 6

—————

**DOCTOR:** How are things with your dad?

**PATIENT:** My life doesn't revolve around him.

**DOCTOR:** Then who *does* your life revolve around?

**PATIENT:** *(Patient doesn't respond.)*

**DOCTOR:** Is that a scar on your arm?

**PATIENT:** Yes.

**DOCTOR:** Something you want to tell me about?

**PATIENT:** Not really.

**DOCTOR:** You aren't trying to hurt yourself, are you?

**PATIENT:** It's an old scar. This is such a waste of time.

**DOCTOR:** Have you thought anymore about hurting other people?

**PATIENT:** *(No response.)*

**DOCTOR:** I'm waiting.

**PATIENT:** *(Still no response.)*

**DOCTOR:** Do you want to talk about something else?

**PATIENT:** I make you uncomfortable, don't I?

**DOCTOR:** What makes you say that?

**PATIENT:** The way your mouth twitches when you ask me a difficult question. The way your jaw tightens when you don't like something I say. You're doing it now . . . with your mouth.

**DOCTOR:** But I'm not asking anything right now.

**PATIENT:** Inside your head you are. You're asking yourself if you can really help someone like me, or if I'm already too far gone. You're asking yourself if someday I might blame you for screwing me up even more, and if I'd ever come back to hurt you.

**DOCTOR:** Those aren't my questions.

**PATIENT:** Do you want to know the answers?

**DOCTOR:** *(Doctor doesn't respond.)*

**PATIENT:** Your jaw is tightening.

**DOCTOR:** Maybe we should end things for today.

**PATIENT:** Just when things were getting interesting.

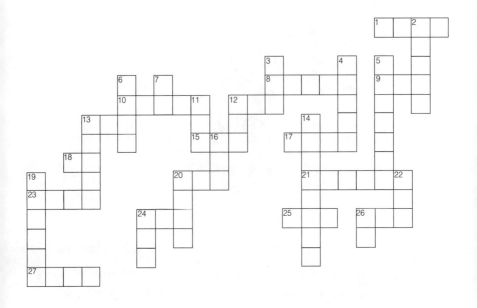

## Across

**27.** Rhymes with moon; the time when I'll reveal myself to you.

# 23

OMPLETELY SHAKEN UP inside, I tell Adam to take me home. On the ride there, he asks me over and over again if I'm okay, and apologizes for trying to get me involved. Part of me wants to tell him the truth about what my aunt and I have sensed. Another part wants to smack him upside the head for not being more concerned about himself than about me.

"You really need to take this seriously," I say, glancing out the window as he turns onto Columbus Street. "Don't be like me—like the way I was."

He asks me to elaborate, but I really don't feel like dredging up the details of what happened with Matt, remembering what it was like to be held captive in the back of a trailer and the haunting sensation of constantly being watched.

"I'm sure there's some stupid explanation," he says, finally turning onto my street.

"Like what?" I ask. "Someone wants you dead."

"There's no need to jump to conclusions."

"Did you not see the same message I did? It said that you deserve to die."

"I'm just trying to be rational here—to put things into perspective." Adam pulls up in front of my house and puts the car in park.

"Then what about the crossword puzzles? You obviously thought they were significant enough to cancel your plans with Piper." I shake my head, thinking how Kimmie had warned me about Adam's sincerity. Does he seriously believe he might be in danger, or was this whole scene tonight just an excuse to see me?

"What do you want me to say?" he asks.

"That you won't go home alone."

"Looking for a little company?" He winks.

"You know what I mean."

"Unfortunately, I do." He sighs.

"Can you call Tray? Or, better yet, campus police? Have them check things out at your apartment."

"I'll call Tray."

"Promise?"

He nods and gazes at my mouth. "It'll give me an excuse to talk to him about stuff."

"Then call me afterward, okay?"

Adam agrees, and I step out of his car, catching a glimpse of Ben's motorcycle parked across the street.

I watch as Adam pulls away, and then look around for Ben, wondering if he's already inside the house. But then

I spot a shadow moving toward me from the end of the street.

"Ben?" I call.

A chill in the air cuts through my core, and I tighten the collar of my coat. Finally I recognize Ben's posture and walk. Wearing dark clothing, he moves beneath one of the streetlamps, and I see his face.

"What are you doing here?" I ask.

"Waiting for you," he says, standing right in front of me now. His eyes are watery from the cold.

"You could've called."

"I did call. Your mom said you were out, and so I tried your cell, but you've got it turned off."

I pull my cell phone out of my pocket to check. "I don't know how that happened," I say, clicking it back on.

"Maybe you turned it off because you were upset with me."

"Maybe," I say, giving him a pointed look.

"For the record, I really did need to help my aunt, but—"

"Forget it," I say, cutting him off. I press myself against his chest and snake my hands beneath his coat.

"But you come first," he whispers, finishing his thought and drawing me close.

I take his hand and lead him inside the house, where my parents are waiting up for me.

"Ben," Dad says, giving me a confused look. After all, it's not every day that I go out with one boy and end up coming home with another. Ben greets my parents, but Dad's eyes remain fixed on mine. "Is everything . . ."

"It's good," I say, finishing his thought, hoping to ease his fatherly concern.

Ben and I head down the hallway to my bedroom, and I shut the door behind us. I show him the crossword puzzles and then tell him about the past couple of hours with Adam.

"It was like what happened with Matt all over again." I glance at my dresser mirror, reminded of the bright red lettering that had been scribbled across it. "I really thought that I could handle this. I thought I was prepared. I mean, it wasn't like I didn't have any warning."

"Give yourself a break," Ben says, sitting beside me on the bed. "It took a long time for me to get used to my psychometric powers, too."

"I just don't know if I can do this. What if I don't want to know the future?"

"It'll get easier."

"When?" My voice quivers. "It took you two years to come out of seclusion."

"That was different," he says, referring to Julie's death. "I won't let anything like that happen to you." He pries the crossword puzzles out of my hands and runs his fingers over the clues.

"Well?" I ask.

"Well, they were all clearly done by the same person."

"Yes, but you can tell that just by looking at them."

"I can feel it, too. I can feel the same impulse in all of them."

"And what impulse is that?"

He shakes his head. "I can't really tell. I'm sensing a lot of your energy."

"Because they were in my pocket."

He nods.

"So, the impulse could be anything. It could be anger; it could be someone just playing a game—"

"It could be a warning." He holds up the WATCH YOUR BACK puzzle.

"I know," I say, feeling a chill rush over my skin. "It's exactly what you sensed when you touched me in the airport."

"Which just proves how connected we are." Ben sets the puzzles down and pulls me close. "Whatever all of this stuff means, I'm here for you. Remember that."

"Even though it concerns Adam?"

"I'm here for *you*," he repeats.

"So, don't leave me tonight, okay?"

At the same moment, there's a knock on my bedroom door. It's like my parents suddenly have extrasensory powers, too. "Camelia?" my mother calls.

I get up to open the door.

"It's time for Ben to get going, okay?" she says. "You both have school tomorrow."

"Of course," Ben says, standing up from the bed.

I look at the clock. It's a little past ten.

Mom leaves us alone to say our good-byes. Keeping

my eyes open, I kiss Ben full on the lips, hoping he gets the message.

Ben nods as if he *does* get it, and then I walk him to the door, tell my parents good night, and head off to bed.

I N MY ROOM, I change into a long T-shirt and flannel shorts and pull my hair out of its twist so that it falls past my shoulders.

A second later, my cell phone rings. I check the ID to see who it is. "Adam?" I answer.

"Yeah, hi, it's me."

"Did you call campus police?"

"I called Tray. I don't have the strength to deal with campus police tonight. After last semester, they're not exactly fans of mine."

"Is Tray there with you now?"

"Yeah, and everything's fine."

"Are you sure?" I ask, tightening my grip on the phone. "Do you think he'd mind staying with you for a little while?"

"Camelia, I'm fine," he insists. "Whoever did this obviously doesn't have a key to my apartment."

"Why is that obvious?"

"Maybe because the writing was done outside my door, and not splashed across my bedroom wall like in the movies."

"Will you call me first thing tomorrow?"

"I must say, if I knew all this creepy stuff was going to elicit this much attention from you, I'd have gotten myself harassed weeks ago."

"Adam, I'm serious."

"I'll call you tomorrow."

We hang up, and about five minutes later, Ben shows up at my window. I open it wide to let him in. He smells like the night—like burning leaves and the promise of snow.

"Sorry I took so long," he says. "I moved my bike a couple blocks away."

"Clever thinking."

"Are you sure you want to do this?" he asks. "Because I feel sort of weird. I mean, your mom told me to leave."

I glance toward my closed bedroom door, feeling a tad guilty. "I just don't want to be alone right now."

"Well, I'll only stay until you fall asleep." His dark gray eyes draw a zigzag line down the center of my face, landing on my lips.

We ease down onto my bed. The window is still open a crack, and the cool air prompts me to burrow beneath the covers.

And to take Ben along with me.

We pull a blanket over us and face one another on my

pillow. Ben runs his fingers along my hip and then rests his hand against my outer thigh—gently, as if I might break.

I can see he's sweating. His forehead is moist. His fingers tremble against my bare skin, but I silently beg him not to pull away. I place my hand over his, feeling his fingers dig into my leg—almost a little too hard—causing me to flinch.

He draws away, but I pull him back. And kiss him again.

I run my fingers under his sweatshirt, over his chest, feeling perspiration there, too.

"No," he whispers, pulling away once more.

"You won't hurt me," I tell him. My entire body aches. I move to snuggle against him, but he sits up, grabs the bottled water from my night table, and takes a sip. I watch the motion in his neck, and feel myself swallow, too.

Ben sets the water back down and looks straight into my eyes. I reach out to touch the scar on his arm—the branchlike lines and the one broken limb—wishing I could climb up inside the strongest part of him.

And never let go.

"Maybe we should slow down a bit," he says.

I run my hand down his hip and stop at his thigh, somehow sensing a mark on his skin. "I want to be close to you," I insist, wishing he could hold me all night without pulling away.

Ben studies me, as if considering the idea for one magical moment. His lip quivers, and his eyes narrow.

But then he merely kisses my forehead. "I want to be close to you, too," he says. "Probably more than you'll ever know."

He lies beside me on the bed, on top of the covers, while I remain beneath them. It's at least a couple of hours before I'm able to fall asleep—before I can stifle this insatiable thirst inside me.

I don't really know when Ben finally nods off, or if he ever does. When I wake up the following morning, he's gone.

# 25

AT SCHOOL THE next day, I can't seem to concentrate in any of my classes. What with everything that's been happening with Adam, and the experience last night with Ben, I feel completely and emotionally spent.

I try to catch Kimmie and Wes up at lunch, filling them in on the words splashed across Adam's door and all the drama going on with his friends, but Kimmie is less than interested, instead zeroing in on what happened with Ben: "So he was actually waiting for you when you got home?" she asks, peeling the lid off her yogurt.

"Was he upset that you were out playing Nancy Drew with Adam?" Wes asks.

"Quite the contrary," I say, feeling my face go pink.

"*Oh, really?*" Kimmie asks, perking up. She gives her yogurt lid a lick. "Details, please."

"Or, better yet, snapshots," Wes says.

"Ben was a total gentleman," I assure them.

"Okay, this respect thing he's got going for you is getting way old," she says. "Of course, you know I'm just jealous. What I wouldn't give to have a hot guy like that respect me."

"Speaking of hot guys and jealousy," I say, "do you think Tray is jealous enough of Adam to think he deserves to die?"

"So, you *do* admit that Adam's hot," Kimmie says, raising her stud-pierced eyebrow at me.

"Not hot, just . . ."

"Smokin'," she blurts out. "I mean, let's face it, the boy's a regular five-alarm fire."

"But it doesn't make sense," Wes says. "Adam and Melissa only went out one time, and it was before Adam even knew that Tray was interested in her."

"We can't all be psychic." Kimmie sighs.

"And, of course, we're only hearing one side of the story," I remind them.

"Well, one date or not, I suspect Melissa might just be psychotic enough to deem Adam maggot-feed-worthy for dumping her," Kimmie says. "I mean, did you not see the way she looked at me yesterday? I swear, her fangs were showing."

Wes shows off his own fangs, having dipped his mouth into a pool of ketchup. "So, what's next?" he asks, doing his best Count Dracula impersonation.

I shrug, suddenly remembering how Adam never called me this morning, even though he said he would. "I should probably go back to Adam's apartment to have a look at his door."

"Want some company?" Wes asks. "I can bring along my spy tools. I've got a cool new UV-light device that picks up all traces of bodily fluids."

"You're kidding, right?" Kimmie asks.

"You know you want to give it a try." He winks. "I'll even let you borrow my latex gloves."

"Say no more," she jokes. "I'm in."

We arrange to meet in the back parking lot after school. Ben shows up, too, about ten cars away. He hops on his motorcycle and looks in my direction.

"I think someone's waiting for you," Wes nudges. "So, why not go say hello?"

"Or better yet, why not hop on his lap and have him drive you to heaven?" Kimmie says. "I mean, honestly, could that boy be any yummier?"

"Wait—what about your dad?" I ask her.

"Um, gross." She makes a face. "You don't seriously think my dad's yummy, do you?"

"No." I giggle. "I mean, you never filled me in on what's going on with him . . . and his new girlfriend."

Kimmie turns to me. Her face is completely serious despite the glitter sprinkled on her cheeks. "You don't really want to interrupt this program to talk about my pedophile of a dad, do you?"

"I assume now's not the right time to discuss him?"

"You assume right," she says, nodding toward Lily

(peace-loving) Randall and her posse of flower-power friends. It's obvious that they're admiring Ben, daring each other to go up and talk to him.

"What's going on?" I ask.

"Ben's getting scoped, that's what," Kimmie says. "And it was only a matter of time. One day a social outcast . . ."

"The next, Freetown High School's hottest flavor," Wes says, finishing her thought. "I overheard some girls in English saying how it's sort of sexy the way he's saved your life, like, ten times now."

"It was actually three times," I say, as if the distinction even matters.

"He's still a hero," Wes says.

"A *super*hero," Kimmie clarifies, "with just the right amount of bad boy to keep him interesting."

At the same moment, a couple of senior girls walk by him. They smile in his direction, but Ben remains focused on me.

"Get over there and mark your touchable territory," Kimmie insists. "Mark it with a detentionworthy kiss."

I make my way over to him, still feeling a bit vulnerable after last night. "Hi," I say, stopping right in front of him. "I missed you today in chemistry."

"I got to school a little late."

"But you left my house early," I say, wondering what time he *did* in fact leave—if he waited until I fell asleep or stayed until the last possible moment.

"I still overslept," he explains.

"I'm sorry if that was my fault."

"I think it *was* your fault." He smiles wider. "Once I got home, I couldn't really fall asleep. Too wound up, I guess."

"Because of all the drama with Adam?"

He shakes his head and touches the side of my face, raising my chin slightly to kiss my lips. "Do you need a ride home?"

I peer over my shoulder at Wes and Kimmie, only to discover that Adam is there, too. He's parked his Bronco in one of the empty spaces. Kimmie and Wes are talking to him through his driver's-side window.

"Looks like I'm not the only one who wants to whisk you away," Ben says.

"Wait here," I say, reluctantly heading over to Adam's car. Kimmie and Wes step aside.

"I'm sorry to bother you," Adam says. "I just didn't know what else to do. I was going to call you, but then I thought you'd want to see it."

"See what?" I ask, noticing how troubled he looks. His neck is splotchy, and all the color has drained from his face.

"Can you talk? Can we go somewhere to discuss everything?"

"Just tell me," I insist. "What's going on?"

"I got another one."

"Another crossword puzzle?"

He nods and reaches into his pocket, unfolds a piece of paper, and hands it to me. It's just like all the other ones. And the message is very clear: *I WANT TO SEE YOU BLEED.*

# 26

*A*DAM WAITS WHILE I tell Kimmie and Wes that I have to go.

"No big deal," Wes says. "We'll break in my UV light another time."

I look back at Ben, knowing that for him it *is* a big deal. The last time Ben really cared for someone, Adam snatched her attention away. And here it's happening again.

I give Kimmie and Wes a hug good-bye, and then I join Ben again. "Adam really needs me right now," I tell him.

"Yeah, I kind of figured." He looks down at his helmet, maybe so I can't see his disappointment.

"I'm sorry," I whisper, wishing there could be some other way.

Ben nods and pulls his helmet on. He revs up his engine and drives away. Meanwhile, Lily Randall's Volkswagen

Bug follows close behind him, creating an uneasy feeling in the pit of my stomach.

I tell Adam to take us to his apartment. We don't really say much on the drive, mostly because I'm far too tense for small talk.

Adam can feel the tension, too: "I'm sorry to pull you away from your friends."

"Forget it," I say, knowing that, as hard as it was to leave Ben, I would've regretted it if I hadn't.

We finally get to Adam's building and climb the stairs to his apartment. To my complete and utter surprise, the writing on his door is gone.

Vanished.

"What happened?" I ask.

It takes him a second before he realizes what I'm asking. "I washed it off," he explains.

"You *what?*"

"I wasn't going to, but I didn't want the super to give me a hard time. Plus, I thought it might freak out some of my neighbors. You have to admit, death threats on doors can be pretty offensive, generally speaking. Not to mention the sheer fact that it made me look like a total asshole—like some old girlfriend was trying to get even."

"Did you take pictures at least?"

"Actually, no." He cringes. "That probably would've been a good idea."

"But Tray saw the writing, right?"

"Um . . ." He nibbles his lip, clearly reading my angst.

"You told me he was with you last night. You said you called him."

"I tried, but he didn't pick up, and I didn't want you to worry."

"So, you lied?" I snap.

"I didn't want you to worry," he repeats. "Please, don't be upset."

"How can I not be? We're talking about your life here. You can't go erasing evidence off your door. And you can't be lying to me, either. How am I supposed to help if you don't tell me the truth?"

"Why *are* you helping me?" he asks, taking a step closer. "I mean, I'm grateful and all, and you know I love spending time with you, be it death-threat missions or pizza and a movie. It's just . . . what do you get out of it? What's this sudden interest in my life?"

My mouth drops open, but I manage a shrug, almost forgetting the fact that he knows nothing about my premonitions.

"What about Ben?" he continues; his brown eyes are piercing. "He can't possibly think it's a good idea for you to get involved with all this . . . to get involved with me."

"Don't worry about Ben."

"Are *you* worried about him? Are you at all concerned about what he might think?"

"Ben trusts me," I say, hoping to put an end to this line of questioning.

"That's good," he says, clearly sensing the sudden

awkwardness between us. He fakes a smile and then turns to unlock the door.

I follow him inside; he stops me at the kitchen island. "I found it right here." He points to the countertop.

"You found *what* right *where*?" I ask, feeling my face scrunch up in bewilderment.

"The crossword puzzle from today." He pulls it out of his pocket. "I found it here when I was making breakfast this morning."

"Wait, you didn't get it in the mail?"

"I'm sorry; I thought I mentioned that."

"No," I say, holding back from whacking him in the head. "I think I would've remembered if someone had broken into your apartment."

"I'm sorry," he repeats, and then lets out a stress-filled sigh.

"So, someone broke in here last night while you were asleep?"

"I'm not sure. I was thinking that, too, but then . . . what if I just didn't see it last night when I got home?"

"Are you sure you didn't set your mail down here, maybe even for a second, and then leave this piece behind?"

"What difference does it make?"

"It makes a huge difference." My voice gets louder. "The difference between someone breaking in or not." I peer around the kitchen and living room, trying to see if anything looks off.

"I don't know." He reaches for a box of cereal. "I mean, I'm pretty sure I would've noticed getting another puzzle in the mail, especially since we've been talking so much about this stuff."

"Who has a key to your apartment?"

"No one that I know of."

"None of your friends? Did you leave a spare under the doormat, maybe?"

"No, and no."

"Then what?" I ask, completely frustrated.

"Look," he says, running his fingers through his shaggy brown hair. "I don't have all the answers. That's why it's a puzzle."

"This isn't funny," I tell him. "Someone's sending you threatening notes, writing twisted messages on your door, and possibly breaking into your apartment. Worrying isn't an option. It's an order."

"So what do you order me to do?"

"Call the police."

"And tell them what? That someone's sending me crossword puzzles? That I got an angry message on my door, but I didn't even feel the need to save it? They'll give me a Breathalyzer test and ask me what I've been drinking."

"At least they'll have it all on record."

Adam nods. But still, he doesn't move.

"What's wrong?" I ask.

He hesitates, shuffling his feet as he snacks from the cereal box. It's a full five seconds before he finally looks into my eyes again. "I really don't feel comfortable bringing this up with you."

"No secrets, remember?"

"Okay," he says, letting out a giant breath. "Do you think Ben could be the one doing this? Maybe he's trying to get me back for everything."

"Seriously?" I ask.

"I mean, I almost wouldn't blame him. It was totally ass of me to try and steal you away from him . . . even to seek him out in the first place, and to come back into his life. It's all so heinous and embarrassing, which is exactly what I told my shrink."

"It isn't Ben," I say, irritated that he could even think so. "Maybe it was Tray. You said yourself that he's jealous of you."

"Tray's my friend. We were good friends before all that BS went down with Melissa."

"You and Ben were good friends once, too," I remind him.

Adam manages a subtle nod. "But that was a long time ago."

"I know Ben, and he wouldn't do this." I give him the CliffsNotes version of what happened between Matt and me. "Ben saw what that did to me—how scared I was and how I didn't know whom to trust."

"All the more reason," he says. "Ben saw how effective the stalking was."

"He also saw how both people got caught. And this person will, too."

"Maybe," he says, continuing to snack.

"What about Melissa?" I ask. "She's angry that you

ended things with her. Maybe this is her way of teaching you a lesson."

"A total possibility. I'm definitely sweet and studly enough to drive a girl literally insane, wouldn't you say?" He flexes his biceps to be funny.

"Can we please try and be serious here?"

"If we must," he says between bites. "But whether it's Ben, Tray, or even Melissa, I really don't feel like getting any of my past and/or present friends in trouble."

"Even if one of them wants to see you bleed?" I nod toward the latest crossword puzzle sitting on the counter.

Adam looks at it and then at me, evidently still trying to decide.

# AUDIO TRANSCRIPT 7

---

**DOCTOR:** Let's talk today about revenge.

**PATIENT:** Why?

**DOCTOR:** What's your take on revenge?

**PATIENT:** Some people deserve it.

**DOCTOR:** Has anyone ever sought revenge on you?

**PATIENT:** My parents. Whenever I did something that upset them, they got me back for it.

**DOCTOR:** Have you ever sought revenge on other people?

**PATIENT:** I suppose.

**DOCTOR:** Are you seeking it now?

**PATIENT:** Right at this moment?

**DOCTOR:** You know what I mean.

**PATIENT:** *(Patient doesn't respond.)*

**DOCTOR:** Is that a difficult question to answer?

**PATIENT:** People are so stupid. They think they've got the whole puzzle figured out, but they're really so far off.

**DOCTOR:** What are you referring to specifically?

**PATIENT:** This, you, everybody. Everybody's just so dumb.

**DOCTOR:** But not you?

**PATIENT:** I'm just trying to see that things are done right.

**DOCTOR:** Are you still trying to protect your friend?

**PATIENT:** Very much so.

**DOCTOR:** And does that mean seeking revenge on someone else?

**PATIENT:** Once again, everyone is just so dumb.

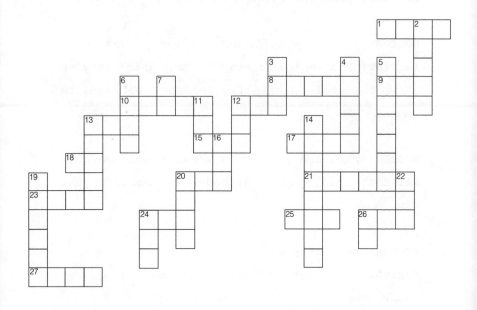

**Across**

**13.** Rhymes with dead; you sleep on it.

**Down**

**4.** Don't forget to _____ behind every corner to see who might be lurking.

**12.** I have all _____ answers.

# 27

*A*FTER ADAM DROPS ME off at home, I sit in my room trying desperately to get through the last few pages of *The Scarlet Letter*. But for some reason, I can't get my mind off Aunt Alexia's journal. It practically stares at me from my night table, as if daring me to touch it.

Finally, I cave in and grab it. I start to flip through a few of the pages, but the phone rings, interrupting me. I click it on, but no one answers when I say hello. "Who's there?" I ask, sitting up in bed.

But somehow I already know the answer.

I can hear someone breathing on the other end. It's a rhythmic, faraway sound that makes my skin itch.

"Aunt Alexia?" I ask; my heart tightens.

A few moments later, the phone clicks as if someone's hung up, and then eventually it goes to a dial tone. I press star-six-nine and scribble the phone number that's given on the edge of a notebook. It's definitely from out of town; I don't recognize the area code or the exchange.

With trembling fingers, I click the receiver back on and dial the number. A voice-mail recording comes on right away: "Hi, this is Haven. Leave me a message, and I'll jingle you right back."

I hang up, beyond disappointed, totally confused, and maybe even a little surprised. Because I have no idea who Haven is (someone with a wrong number, or who likes to make random prank phone calls?). And because my gut really told me the call was from Aunt Alexia.

My adrenaline surging, I grab the most recent crossword puzzle and venture down to my studio, hoping to relax—to take my mind off things by sculpting something meaningful. But I can't really concentrate. I run my fingers over the crossword's paper, hoping for a little inspiration. But nothing comes to mind.

No specific images.

No voices in my head.

Nothing extraordinary whatsoever.

I set the puzzle back down and continue to wedge out my ball of clay. Twenty minutes later, with my fingers waterlogged and my hands cold and clammy, I'm no closer to finding out the answers than I was before I started.

I glance over at my tile pieces from the other day. They're almost fully dry now. I spend several moments arranging the tiles so they form an exact replicate of the crossword puzzle. Then I grab a carving tool and begin filling in all the clues we have so far.

The sight of some of my predictions—of the precise number of tile squares, and the overall shape of the crossword puzzle, not to mention the YOU DESERVE TO DIE clue etched out on several of the tiles—is almost invigorating. It almost makes me begin to embrace this power I have.

So how come I can't get that power to work now?

I cover my work with a plastic tarp. A second later, the phone rings again, making me jump. Only, this time it's my cell, buzzing from inside my pocket.

"How did things go with Adam?" Kimmie asks, as soon as I pick up.

"It's all so confusing."

"Only to you it is. Wes and I tend to see things a whole lot clearer than you do. And, as luck would have it, he just happens to be here with me, hiding out from his dad. So why don't you get your confused ass over here, too?"

"Why is he hiding out?"

"Because his dad paid Helga to come on to him."

"Helga the cleaning lady?"

"Believe it. That woman may be sixty years old and carry her teeth around in a Dixie cup, but apparently she still has game."

"Heinous."

"To put it mildly. So, are you coming over or what?"

"I'll be there," I say, snapping my phone shut. I climb the basement stairs to the kitchen, where my mother is preparing dinner. Dad's helping out by dicing up some raw potatoes.

"Better wash up," Mom says. "We'll be eating in a few minutes."

I glance toward her mixing bowl, in which she's blending something resembling Cat Chow.

Dad grimaces at the sight of it. "What do you say, Camelia?" he says. "Maybe after dinner you and I can head over to Flick-tastic to rent a couple videos?" Translation: *Let's save ourselves from this swill by hitting the drive-through of Taco Bell.*

"Actually, Kimmie just called," I say, breaking the news to him. "Wes is having some major drama with his dad and they asked me to come over."

They both study me for a couple of seconds, as if trying to decide whether or not to let me go, but then Mom gestures toward her keys. "You can take my car. Just promise you'll be home by nine. School tomorrow."

"Thanks," I say, noticing Mom's monogrammed pendant. Her name—Jilly—is written on it in a pretty gold cursive. Aunt Alexia sent it to her for Christmas, and Mom's been wearing it ever since. "Have you spoken to Aunt Alexia or her doctors since our visit?" I ask.

Mom nods and continues to mash her mush.

"*And?*" I ask, when she doesn't elaborate.

"And it's a long story that we can discuss at some other time."

I look at Dad to see if he might have some answers, but he shakes his head slightly, implying the subject is definitely taboo.

"What's wrong?" I persist.

"Go along to Kimmie's," Mom says. "We can talk about it later." She turns her back on me, gobbles a giant spoonful of almond butter—her edible vice—and then chases it with a shiny green pill—something her therapist claims will soothe her, even though it never does.

I linger a few more seconds, but Mom doesn't turn around.

"I haven't forgotten about that calculus assignment you asked me about," Dad fibs. "How about after you get back I give you a hand with it?"

More code. This time he's suggesting that we have one of our heart-to-heart chats tonight, whereby he'll clue me in as to what's going on with Mom.

"Sounds good," I say, and grab Mom's keys, annoyed that she continues to keep secrets from me, while I'm expected to tell her everything.

# 28

*A*BOUT FIVE MINUTES LATER, I arrive at Kimmie's, where she and Wes are camped out on the floor of her room amid remnants of denim and pleather.

"Don't laugh at my outfit," she says, referring to her perfectly pressed chino pants, her powder blue crewneck sweater, and her tan leather loafers. Kimmie's hair, as well, is much tamer than usual, one side held back with a coordinating blue barrette. "It's sort of a long story, and I really don't feel like getting into it."

"And how are *you* doing?" I ask Wes, noting his pink-striped shirt and leather clogs—no doubt the ammo that set his dad off.

"In some way I almost feel bad for my dad." He shrugs. "I'm his worst nightmare come true."

"You're hardly a nightmare," I counter. "Your dad's an ass for not seeing what an amazing person you are."

"Well, then, I'm an amazing person with a friend who's on the road to getting herself killed." He lowers his glasses to glare at me over the rims.

"What are you talking about?" I ask him.

"Wes and I got talking about all this Adam stuff," Kimmie explains for him. "And maybe getting involved isn't such a good idea. I mean, haven't you already been through enough?"

"And what if Ben had shared that same philosophy?" I ask them. "What if last September he'd just decided to look the other way when all of that stuff was happening with Matt? I wouldn't be able to forgive myself if something bad happened to Adam because I did nothing to try and stop it."

"Yes, but you don't even know if Adam's telling you the truth," she says.

"What does Ben say about all this?" Wes asks.

"Because you know it's only a matter of time before he tries convincing you to stop helping Adam," Kimmie says, before I can answer. "And you can't really blame the guy. He isn't going to want you putting yourself in danger again."

"Nor is he going to want you spending all your free time with Adam," Wes adds. "And that's what you're going to have to do, you know, if you really want to figure this all out."

"Don't you think I *should* figure it out?" I ask. "I mean, there's a reason this is happening to me—that I've been given this insight. Shouldn't I use it?"

"Not if it means getting yourself killed," Wes says.

I shake my head, knowing that I haven't even told them the worst of it yet. And so I spend the next several minutes filling them in on the details of the latest cross-word puzzle, and how Adam suspects that someone broke into his apartment.

"And nobody else has a key?" Kimmie asks.

"What about his ex-roommate?" Wes suggests.

"Good question," I say.

"Well, here's a better one," he continues. "What kind of lock is on the door?"

"What difference does that make?"

"It makes a huge difference in the scheme of breaks-ins. For example, is there a dead bolt? And if so, is it surface-mounted, lockset, or maybe a combination of both? Is the lock spring-loaded? Or is it the mortise kind, with a box? On second thought, considering what an ass-pit the place is, my guess is it's a cheapo entry style, just waiting to get picked, but we should probably check it out just to be sure."

"Or we could simply call the police and ask them to do their job," Kimmie says.

"Adam's against calling the police," I say. "He doesn't think we have enough proof. Plus he hates the idea of getting anyone in trouble, especially if it's one of his friends."

"Even if one of his friends wants to kill him?" Wes asks.

"I know," I say. "It's crazy."

"Well, crazy or not, it sounds all too familiar." She gives me the evil eye.

"So, let's go check out the lock," Wes says. "At least then we'll know what kind of talent we're dealing with."

"But first . . ." Kimmie drops a first-prize ribbon into my lap, the gold part of which reads: GRAND PRIZE: VINTAGE REVISITED.

"What's this?" I ask, fairly certain she would have mentioned having entered a contest.

"It's Kimmie's lame-o attempt at getting her parents back together." Wes yawns.

"Explain, please," I say, noticing that the ribbon was awarded by the Fashion Institute.

"Okay, so obviously it isn't legit," she confesses, plucking it out of my hands. "But my parents totally think it is, and as my reward I've told them I want to go out to dinner with just the two of them Saturday night."

"Kimmie will arrange to meet them at the restaurant," Wes explains. "But then she won't bother showing up, leaving Mommy and Daddy to dine on their own."

"Don't you think that's just a tad bit cheesy?" I ask her.

"Not to mention desperate and predictable," Wes adds. "Which is exactly what I told her."

"Well, I really don't see what my alternative is." She huffs. "I've already tried dressing boring . . . like you"—she gestures at my jeans and T-shirt—"and that didn't catch their attention. And you know I went the whole hickey route a few weeks ago, and *that* was a total bust. . . ."

"You don't seriously think their separation is as shallow as a wardrobe malfunction, do you?" I ask her.

"You guys don't understand," she whines. "Everything's different now that they've separated. My mom got a job at the hardware store downtown."

"The horror of it all," Wes jokes.

"Is your mom still drinking a lot?" I ask her.

"It seems she's replaced drinking with working."

"Well, that's better, at least."

"Not for Nate it isn't. He has to go to the Y now every day after school. Meanwhile, Dad's living a bachelor-pad life whilst dating someone barely old enough to vote."

"But maybe they're all happy," Wes says. "I mean, for once your house is quiet. I can't remember the last time I was here that it didn't sound like a filming of *The Texas Chainsaw Massacre*."

"They only *think* they're happy," Kimmie says, sulking. "Things were so much better when they were trying to tear each other's heads off."

*A*FTER KIMMIE SLIPS into something a bit more *her* (a long taffeta skirt paired with a T-shirt and boots), we hop into Wes's car, and he drives us over to Adam's apartment.

"Do you think I should call and tell him we're here?" I ask, looking up at his building.

"No way," Kimmie says. "You'll get way more accomplished with an unannounced visit, which is precisely what I plan to do this weekend. Picture this: me, dropping by my dad's place around eleven p.m. on a Friday night, probably just after he and that child get back from dinner. Any wagers as to what they'll be up to?"

"Why are you trying to punish yourself?" Wes asks.

"It's *him* I'm trying to punish. Can you imagine how pissed he'll be when I tell him I want to spend the night?"

"Let's go," Wes says, grabbing a screwdriver, a rag, and some wire from his glove compartment.

"What, no power drill?" Kimmie asks.

"Are you kidding?" He winks. "My power drill comes with me wherever I go." He pulls on some black leather gloves, and we head up to Adam's floor.

I shake my head at the sight of his door, still stunned that Adam would wash the message away.

Wes tries to pick up any lingering inky residue with his rag, but it comes away pretty clean. "I should've brought along my UV light."

"Because it's superimportant for us to know if the psycho in question peed, drooled, or bled on his door," Kimmie says.

"I guess I can sort of understand why he washed it," Wes continues. "I wouldn't want the world to know that I deserved to die, either."

"Right, but it makes showing the police a whole lot harder," I say.

Wes knocks a couple of times, but Adam doesn't answer. "Jackpot," he says, kneeling down to examine the lock. He takes the bundle of wire from his pocket and proceeds to make a key of sorts.

"You're not going to break in, are you?" I ask.

"Well, um, *yeah*." Kimmie rolls her eyes, as if the answer's completely obvious.

Wes sticks his key into the lock and starts to jiggle it back and forth. A moment later, the doorknob turns.

Only, Wes isn't the one turning it.

Piper then whips the door open. "Oh, my God," she says, smacking her chest like we've scared her, too.

"We were looking for Adam." I peek past her into the apartment.

"He isn't here," she says, glaring at Wes, no doubt annoyed that he's attempting to pick the lock.

"Would you believe that I dropped a contact?" he asks, before finally getting up.

"Not likely, since you're wearing glasses." Kimmie bops him on the head with her Tupperware purse.

"Wait, did you and Adam have a date?" Piper asks me. "Because I totally don't want to be in the way."

"Adam and I are just friends," I tell her.

"Oh, I just thought . . ." She shrugs. "I mean, he doesn't normally blow me off, especially when we're working on a project together."

"He didn't blow you off. We just had some important stuff to discuss."

"Like what?" she asks with a fold of her arms, reminding me of an overprotective parent.

I blink hard, surprised at her attempt to pry.

"Is that why you're here now?" she asks when I don't say a thing.

"Why are *you* here?" I ask.

Piper's face softens, and she unfolds her arms. "My computer's being fixed, so Adam said I could use his. I have a major philosophy paper to finish by tomorrow morning. Does anyone know anything about existentialism?"

"Just that people who practice it think that death is absurd." Kimmie pushes past Piper to step inside the apartment.

"Pretty wacked-out theory, right?" Piper laughs. She nods toward the wire in Wes's hands and then twists the knob back and forth. "No need to try and break in, by the way. It was never even locked. Adam hardly ever locks his door."

"Excuse me?" I ask. My mouth falls open.

"It's true," she says, stepping aside as Wes enters the apartment. "And it's so totally stupid. I've told Adam, like, a *kagillion* times. Tray's place got broken into just a few months back, and he *always* locks up."

I take a deep breath, wondering what else Adam's failed to tell me.

"Yeah, Adam's definitely not the brightest bulb in the socket when it comes to practicality," she continues. "But he's totally sweet. I mean, who else would let me take over his computer for the entire night, right? Certainly not Melissa. Talk about a bad mood. That girl has had her panties in butt-cracker territory for *way* longer than I'd ever have imagined. Ohmygosh, did that just sound totally bitchy?" She covers her mouth. "I'm telling you, I can be *such* a major meanie at times."

"Does she also hang out here when Adam's not home?" I ask.

"We all do," she says, scrunching up her bobbed black hair with her hands. "Adam's supergenerous with his place, which is extra good for me, seeing as I still live at home."

I shake my head, completely confused. I mean, how are we supposed to figure all of this out if Adam isn't taking it seriously enough to lock up? "Did you happen to see the writing on his door?"

"What writing?" She cocks her head to one side.

"Forget it." I sigh.

"Better to ask Tray, maybe. He and Janet were here just before I arrived. And you should totally have seen them, too. *So* supercute. I wish he'd just ask her out."

"Why doesn't he?" Wes asks.

"Stupidity?" She giggles. "Seriously, boys don't know what they want."

"Amen to that," Kimmie says, rifling through Adam's kitchen cabinets.

"Are you thirsty?" Piper asks, watching as Kimmie pretends to search for a glass.

Meanwhile, Wes is drawing something on Adam's dry-erase board. It's a hangman puzzle, complete with a stick figure hanging from a noose. Wes fills in the message over the dashed letter spaces: IDIOT, LOCK YOUR DOOR!

## 30

*A*FTER OUR IMPROMPTU visit to Adam's apartment, Wes takes me back to Kimmie's house so I can get my mom's car and drive home.

"Looks like you'll make it just in time for your curfew," he says, checking the clock.

Kimmie breathes a heart-shaped cloud onto the passenger-side window. "I can't even remember the last time a curfew meant anything in my house."

"I have a curfew," Wes chirps, "but my dad respects me more when I blow it."

"Which is why you're going to help me with my precalc homework tonight," Kimmie says, turning to him.

"Sadly, that would have to be the sexiest offer I've gotten in a long time."

"Even sexier than Helga the cleaning lady?" I joke.

"Of course, you're so full of fungus," Kimmie tells

him. "Rumor has it that Tiffany Bunkin has *major* hot pants for you."

"Well, I suppose that's better than granny pants," he says. "But you seem to be forgetting that Tiffany Bunkin smells like dirt and looks like a dandelion."

"That's her charm," Kimmie sings. "She's one of those earthy-crunchy tree-hugging girls."

"An earthy-crunchy tree-hugging girl who dyes her hair yellow and spikes it up to look like petals," he adds.

"Tiffany is totally cute," I tell him.

"And you should totally ask her out," Kimmie says.

"She's already asked *me* out," he says.

"Aren't we one for secrets? So, what did you tell her?" I ask.

"Just that I'd have to check my schedule."

"Why?" Kimmie glares at him. "Because you might have a *CSI* marathon to catch or some ugly shoes to shop for?"

"I just don't think that Tiffany's my type."

"Well, then, who *is* your type?"

"Maybe we should let Wes make his own dating decisions," I suggest.

"Yeah, but what fun would that be?" Kimmie says. "Especially since I haven't gotten any of my own offers in, like, even longer than Wes's hair." She attempts to run her hand through his lengthy layers, but her fingers get caught up in the gel.

"Good night," I tell them, rechecking the clock. I have less than nine minutes to get home before my parents start to panic.

* * *

Exactly seven minutes later, I pull into my driveway, and the motion detector goes on right away.

Illuminating Ben.

The light shines on his perfectly chiseled features, his broad chest, and a sudden sprinkling of snow as it falls all around him.

"What are you doing here?" I ask, stepping out of the car.

"Waiting for you." He closes the car door behind me. "I called you earlier and your mom said you'd be home around nine. You're two minutes early."

"Should I go away and come back?"

"What do *you* think?" he asks, encircling my waist with his arms. Snowflakes land on his face, making his skin glisten.

"You know, you could always ring the doorbell. My parents would let you wait inside."

"Next time." He kisses my lips; his mouth is wet with snow. "So, how was your day?"

"It's a long story," I say, taking his hand and leading him toward my bedroom window. "Wait here."

"What happened to being honest with your parents?"

I clench my teeth, still bitter that my mom wouldn't tell me about Aunt Alexia earlier. While Ben waits for me to let him in, I enter through the front door. My dad's doing bills at the living room table, and my mother's making banana pops in the kitchen.

"Have a nice time, sweetie?" she asks.

"It was fine," I say, almost eager for her to ask about Wes—to see how plugged in to my world she actually is.

"Well, that's good," she says instead.

"Did you talk to Aunt Alexia tonight?"

She shakes her head and dips a pop into a bowl filled with carob and nuts. "I'm going to freeze these overnight. They should be good and ready by tomorrow morning."

"Sounds great," I say, deciding to remain secretive, too. I move into the living room and ask Dad if I can take a rain check on our heart-to-heart.

"Are you sure?" he asks, removing his glasses. His eyes look tired and strained.

"Tomorrow," I promise. "I kind of just want to go to bed."

He nods and kisses me good night, confessing that he, too, is beyond exhausted.

In my room, I close and lock my door, then open my window wide to let Ben in. He shakes the snow from his hair, but he's completely covered.

"Here," I say, helping him off with his coat and his sweatshirt, until there's only a thin layer of T-shirt covering his chest. "You must be freezing." I use the corner of my blanket to wipe his face dry.

"Quite the contrary." He takes my hands and pulls me onto the bed, into his lap, still expecting me to fill him in on all the details.

And so I do.

But Wes couldn't have been more right.

"I really don't like the idea of someone having the

potential to break in to Adam's place," he says. "It definitely makes this all the more dangerous."

"Not if Adam failed to lock his door, and if he promises to keep it locked from now on." I look down at our hands, clasped together, feeling sure that there's something he's not telling me. "Are you sensing something right now?"

"About Adam?" He smirks. "Not exactly."

"Then about me?" I swallow hard.

Instead of answering, Ben opens my hand and runs his thumb along the center of my palm, sending tingles straight down my spine. "What do you think would happen if we combined forces?"

"I'm not sure I understand."

"Any chance your parents are in bed yet?" He peers out my window at the snow flurries. "It's not like I'd be able to ride home in this weather anyway."

We wait for my parents to turn in and shut their bedroom door, and then we sneak downstairs to the basement. I click on my worktable lamp but keep the overhead lights turned off. Instead, I light a vanilla bean candle. The flame's shadow dances against the wall, making the snowflakes that land against the window appear almost shimmery.

"Will your aunt be wondering where you are?" I ask.

Ben shakes his head and rolls up his sleeves, exposing his scar. "She pretty much gives me free rein."

"You're lucky."

"I don't know." A lock of hair falls over his eye. "Sometimes it's nice to have someone waiting up for you."

"Did your parents used to wait up?"

"My mom did. My dad was always too busy."

"Do you still talk to them much?"

"At least a couple times a month. I talk to my mother, mostly. My dad and I have always had our issues." He looks down at his scar, perhaps suddenly self-conscious. "What happened with Julie only made things worse."

"Because he blamed you?"

He shrugs. "He never really said either way, but he was definitely disappointed."

"That must have been hard," I say, wishing I could've been there for him.

"Yeah, I was pretty messed up about it. I started meeting with a therapist, but it was only for a short period of time, because even she didn't support me."

"I'm sorry," I say, reaching out to touch his scar, and feeling how truly wounded he still is.

"So, shall we get down to business?" he asks, nodding toward my worktable.

I lift the pieces of tarp to show him my crossword tiles, and how I've etched in some of the clues.

Ben looks at Adam's most recent crossword puzzle— the one that says *I WANT TO SEE YOU BLEED* lying open on my work board. He picks it up and presses it between his palms. I watch as he closes his eyes and concentrates hard. His hands quiver slightly, and the paper crinkles up.

"What do you sense?" I ask.

"You," he whispers.

"Because it was with my pottery stuff?"

"I guess. . . . I'm not really sure."

"So, let's get started," I say.

Ben stands just behind me, and we begin to wedge out a fresh piece of clay. I try my best to concentrate, to ignore the fact that my heart is beating at five times its normal speed. I watch his arms as he kneads the clay—almost a little too hard—and as the muscles in his forearms flex. "That's good," I say, in an effort to stay focused. I dip a sponge into a bowl of water and squeeze the droplets down over his hands to keep things moist.

After several minutes, Ben lets me take the lead. I place my palms over the clay mound and close my eyes. Meanwhile Ben's chest grazes my shoulders, and his clay-soaked fingers stroke the length of my arms.

"You're doing great," he whispers in my ear.

We continue to sculpt for another hour, working the mound down into a flattened surface—until we have a total of four tiles.

And until I can no longer hold myself back.

I turn around to face him.

"Camelia?" He squints slightly.

I bite my lip, wishing that he could read my mind, and that he would kiss me until my lips ache. "What are you thinking?" I ask, slipping my hand inside the waistband of his jeans and pulling him closer.

His mouth trembles, but he doesn't answer, and so I turn back to our work. A jumble of emotion swims inside me—need, disappointment, embarrassment, frustration—

and my eyes suddenly sting. Still, I glide my fingers over the surfaces of the tiles, confident about the word that fits inside. It plays in my mind's ear. I can see it in my mind's eye. It's like a flashing neon sign that makes my head throb.

"Soon," I whisper, writing the letters using the tip of my finger. I look at my clay replica of the crossword puzzle, somehow confident about where the word fits. I remove the four tiles at the lower left—the horizontally placed ones that help make up the capital *L* shape—and replace them with these tiles. Then I turn back to Ben, eager for his response.

"Stay out of it," he says.

"Excuse me?"

"Stay out of what's going on with Adam, I mean. It isn't safe."

"How can you say that?" I ask. "I mean, you, of all people, should understand what I'm feeling."

"I *do* understand."

"So, then, where is all of this coming from? Why does the word *soon* suddenly change things? This person still wants to see Adam bleed; he still thinks that Adam deserves to die. . . ."

"I know."

"Then, what?" I ask; my voice gets louder. "Because I feel like you're not telling me everything." I look up at the door that leads to the kitchen, hoping I haven't awakened my parents.

Ben studies my face for five full seconds, noticing

maybe how red my eyes are, how flushed my face is. "Just trust me on this," he says.

"On what?" I snap, keeping my voice low.

"On the fact that I'm trying to protect you. That I'm trying to protect us and our relationship."

"You can't do this," I insist. "You can't go on leaving me out. This is my relationship, too."

"It's *our* relationship."

"So how come lately I feel like you're the only one in it—calling all the shots, playing with my head?" I think of all the times he's shown up on a whim—at my house, at my bedroom window, in the parking lot at school, and when I was on my way back from Detroit—only to pull away, leaving me confused.

"I'm sorry," he says, nearly choking on the words. "But believe me when I say that I never meant to hurt you. That's what I've been trying to avoid all along." He reaches out to take my hand, but it's way too little and far too late.

And so, for once, it's me who pulls away.

"I really think you should go," I tell him. There's a crumbling sensation inside my heart.

Ben's eyes are red, too, now, but he still doesn't argue. Instead he gives me a paltry peck on the cheek, and then heads out the bulkhead door.

# AUDIO TRANSCRIPT 8

**DOCTOR:** What do you have there?

**PATIENT:** What does it look like?

**DOCTOR:** A pen. Some paper.

**PATIENT:** Let me guess: did you graduate with honors?

**DOCTOR:** High honors, if you must know. What are you writing?

**PATIENT:** Soon.

**DOCTOR:** Soon what?

**PATIENT:** Soon, I'll get what I want. Soon, things will be as they should.

**DOCTOR:** What *do* you want? How *should* they be?

**PATIENT:** *(Patient doesn't respond.)*

**DOCTOR:** Can I see your notebook?

**PATIENT:** *(No response.)*


**DOCTOR:** Is that a crossword puzzle you're doing?
See, I knew you liked puzzles. And how are you
doing at finding the answers?

**PATIENT:** Great. Really, really great.

31

*A*FTER BEN LEAVES, I head back upstairs to my room, only to find Dad in the kitchen. He has his back toward me, sneaking a bag of Bugles from one of the baskets above the cabinets.

"Caught you," I say, switching on the light, making him jump.

"Shouldn't you be in bed?" he asks, keeping his voice low.

"Shouldn't you?" I give him a pointed look.

"Probably, but your mom actually fell asleep tonight— probably the first night all week. Meanwhile, I'm too hungry to nod off."

"So, where does that leave us?" I ask, eyeing his bag of Bugles.

"Can you be trusted?"

"That depends. Are you willing to share?" I smile. "Good hiding spot, by the way. Nobody ever uses those baskets."

"That's what *you* think." He gazes down the hall to make sure the coast is clear and then snags a bag of Hershey's Kisses from one of the other four overhead baskets.

We park ourselves at the kitchen island and rip both bags open. Five full minutes of lusty devouring pass before either of us speaks.

"I wanted to talk to you about earlier," he says. "About Aunt Alexia. Apparently, her treatment isn't working so well."

I pop a Kiss-stuffed Bugle into my mouth. "That facility isn't the right place for her. I've even told Mom so."

Dad stops chewing and studies my face, curious, maybe, as to why I'm so convinced. "Aunt Alexia got into some trouble tonight," he tells me. "Shortly after you left for Wes's, Mom got a call from the director of the facility. Alexia stole a nurse's cell phone and tried to make a call."

I close my eyes, thinking about the phone call I got earlier. "Do you know the nurse's name?"

Dad resumes eating as he thinks about it a moment. "Haven," he says, between chews.

"Haven," I repeat, standing up from the stool. My face gets hot, and my mind starts to scramble. I replay the voice-mail recording in my head, sure now that it was Alexia who called me earlier tonight.

"Is something wrong?" Dad asks, reaching out to touch my arm.

I shake my head and sit back down.

"According to your mom," Dad continues, "Alexia feels different somehow—misunderstood and at the same time more intuitive than anyone else around her."

"Intuitive?"

He nods and continues to study me. "She says she's able to sense things about the future. Can you imagine what that must be like?"

My eyes betray me by filling with tears. I look away, down into my palms, suddenly feeling as if it's me who's going crazy.

Dad gives my forearm a squeeze and asks again if something's wrong.

But I honestly have no words.

Tears course down the sides of my face, and yet I have no idea what I'm crying about anymore—if it's for Aunt Alexia, or my relationship with Ben, if it's for everything that Kimmie and Wes are going through with their parents . . . Maybe it's just for me.

Dad allows me to crumple up in his arms. He holds me for several minutes before escorting me to my bedroom and tucking me into bed. "Is there anything you want to talk about?" he asks.

"I'm tired," I whisper, rolling away so he can't see my face.

"You'll feel better after some rest," he says, kissing me on the temple. "And don't you worry about your aunt. Everything will work out fine in the end. It always does." He moves her journal from my pillow, placing it on my bedside table without so much as asking where it came from. Without so much as a hint of surprise that it even exists.

# 32

*J*LIE IN BED, my head full of questions; the word SOON is lit up behind my eyes, making my head ache. I glance over at Aunt Alexia's journal, noting how the pages are yellowed; how the cover's been torn, patched over, and torn again; and how Alexia's name is emblazoned across the front in thick black marker.

Is it possible that Dad didn't notice what it was?

Unable to fall asleep, I grab my cell phone to get Kimmie's take on things, including my recent blowout with Ben, but before I can even dial, it rings.

"Hey," Adam says when I answer. "I'm sorry to call so late."

I check the clock. It's a little before midnight. "Is everything okay?" I catch my reflection in the dresser mirror, noticing right away how tired I look. The skin beneath my eyes is bluish gray, and my hair looks matted and dull.

"I got another one," he says.

"Where?" I ask. My head throbs.

"On my windshield. I was at the library for a couple hours. When I got back out to my car, it was there, folded up in an envelope."

"And what did it say?" I ask, almost expecting to hear him tell me, "*Soon.*"

"Check the bed." His voice cracks saying the words.

"Excuse me?"

"That's what it said."

"And what's it supposed to mean?"

"Call me crazy, but I think it might mean that I should check my bed."

"Not funny."

"Who's laughing? I'm paranoid about going home now. I'm having major flashbacks to summer camp. You know, itching powder in the bedsheets, snakes under the pillow, getting your hand dipped into a bowl full of water while you sleep—"

"You've started locking your door, right?"

"Yeah. I mean, mostly."

"Which one is it, yeah or mostly?"

Adam lets out a sigh, making the answer pretty obvious.

"I just don't get it," I tell him. I mean, if he's so concerned about his safety, if he's really as nervous as he's making himself out to be, he'd be locking his door. Every time.

"Say something."

"Were you alone at the library?" I ask.

"Initially, but then I saw Tray and Janet. Melissa was there, too. We all just sort of bumped into one another."

"And did *they* see the crossword puzzle? Have you even asked any of them if they've been receiving these puzzles, too?"

"I asked Piper."

"And?"

"And she had no idea what I was talking about," he says.

"So, where are you now?"

"Driving around, talking to you. I just passed the Press & Grind. God, I wish they were open right now."

"Come and get me."

"Camelia—no. It's way too late. I'm sorry I even bothered you."

"Come now," I insist, pulling on my coat. The word SOON still flashes before my eyes. "We don't have much time."

# 33

CRAWL OUT OF MY bedroom window and meet
Adam at the end of my street.

"I hope I'm not getting you in trouble," he
says, once I'm inside his car.

"Is that the puzzle?" I ask, ignoring his comment,
eager to get down to business. I grab the envelope from
the dashboard and unfold the paper inside. Adam's filled
in the letter blocks; the words CHECK THE BED scream up
at me in bold black letters.

Adam turns toward me. His eyes are wide, and his face
looks slightly sweaty. "So, what do you think?"

"I think we'd better go check your bed."

He swallows hard, seemingly surprised. "For real?"

I nod, and he reluctantly puts the car in drive, pulls
away from the curb, and heads toward his apartment.

"Did you tell anyone that you were coming out with
me?" he asks.

"Of course," I lie, feeling like an idiot for failing to tell a single soul, especially since he's duped me in the past. "I called Kimmie and Ben."

"And what did they say?"

"That they're giving me an hour, tops, before they come looking for me and/or calling the police."

"That's a pretty protective posse you've got there."

"It is," I agree, gazing out at the street. I rest my hand on the cell phone in my pocket, relieved to know it's there.

About fifteen minutes later, Adam pulls into the parking lot at the back of his apartment building. But instead of going around to the front, he leads us down a narrow alley, insisting that we use the side entrance.

"It's quicker," he says, opening the door for me.

The entryway is almost completely unlit except for one low-watt bulb that hangs down from the center of the ceiling, illuminating a dank and tiny space.

"Are you sure this is the way?" I ask, startled by how dark it is.

"I live here, remember?" He smiles and opens the stairwell door, sticking close by my side.

We climb the two flights to his floor and then stand outside his apartment. Adam looks more nervous than I've ever seen him before. He fumbles for the right key.

"What's wrong?" I ask, aware that he's stalling. I look at my watch. It's well past midnight now.

"I just don't know what I'm doing," he says.

"Why? What do you mean?"

He shrugs. His jaw is visibly clenched. And he looks

almost as fragile as I did a few months ago. "I shouldn't have brought you here," he whispers.

At the same moment, there's a creaking sound, like someone's walking nearby on the floor. I peer down the hall, but I don't see anyone.

"I mean, what the hell am I doing bringing someone I really care about into a messed-up situation like this?" he continues.

"I care about you, too," I say, reaching out to touch his hand. "That's *why* I'm here."

Adam clasps my fingers, but he doesn't quite look me in the eye now. "I should've called Tray. It's just . . . I don't know. It's like I don't know who I can trust anymore."

I nod, knowing exactly how he feels. "You can trust *me*," I say, almost able to hear Kimmie's cynical voice inside my head, telling me that this is Adam's ploy—that he's acting all vulnerable just to gain my trust and sympathy, and that I'd be better off walking away.

But instead I squeeze his hand tighter and remind him that the police are just a phone call away. "They could escort us inside. We could turn everything over to them right here. Right now."

"Not yet."

"Then when?"

Adam shrugs again. "I don't know. I don't have all the answers."

"Hence the puzzle," I say, trying to make him smile.

It works. His face brightens slightly, but still . . . He looks almost as remorseful as that night about a month ago, when he told me how much he cared about me. When he realized what a big mistake he'd made by seeking me out as a way to get revenge on Ben.

"I should take you home," he says.

"No," I say, pulling him closer to the door. I try the knob, relieved when it doesn't turn.

Adam unlocks the door; it makes a deep clicking sound that cuts right through my core. A moment later, I hear more creaking noises from down the hall. I turn to look just as Adam ushers me inside the apartment and locks the door behind us.

"When was the last time you were here?" I ask.

"Around dinnertime. I went to the library after that."

"Did you see Piper?"

"Just for a second," he says, looking toward his bedroom. "Oh, right, she mentioned you'd stopped by."

Instead of asking me what I'd wanted, he moves in the direction of his open bedroom door. "I might as well get this over with, right?" he asks. "Like ripping off a Band-Aid?"

I follow close behind him, my cell phone clenched in my hand. From just inside the doorway, his room looks completely normal. I move to the foot of the bed.

"So what now?" Adam asks before venturing toward his bed pillows. With shaking hands, he checks beneath them. "Nothing," he says with a smile of relief.

I smile, too.

Adam takes a deep breath and grabs a corner of the comforter. He pulls it off in one quick motion. The word *SOON* is painted across his bedsheet in bloodred letters.

## 34

*A*T LUNCH THE FOLLOWING DAY, I fill Kimmie and Wes in on everything that went down at Adam's the previous night.

"And no one's called the police yet?" Kimmie asks.

"Why are you surprised?" Wes checks his newly coiffed Elvis sideburns in the mirror stuck to his lunch box. "It's not like Chameleon called the police when all that stalker stuff was happening to *her*."

"Not surprised, just annoyed." She shoots me an evil look. "So maybe you and Adam are perfect together after all."

"Not perfect. Just paranoid."

"Apparently not paranoid enough," she says, dipping a corner of her muffin into a container of jelly. "I mean, what will it take before he finally makes that call?"

"Actual bloodshed on his bed?" Wes suggests. "A knife pressed against his gut?"

"Or rat poison in his fruit juice, maybe?" Kimmie asks.

"Adam's picking me up from school again today," I tell them.

"To have a closer look at his bedsheets?" Wes winks.

"More like to discuss all the clues in this whole convoluted puzzle," I say, ignoring his attempt at humor.

"P.S.," Kimmie segues, tugging on her lip ring, "you have to admit: it's sort of romantic that you and Ben were able to combine forces and do that tile sculpture together."

"Romantic in a stalker-bludgeoning-bedsheets sort of way," Wes says to clarify.

"And my guess as to why Ben got all weird and protective on you, postsculpture," she continues, "is that he sensed something significant."

"He *did* sense something," I say, nodding. "He just wouldn't tell me what that something was. He said that by not telling me, he was protecting me *and* our relationship."

"Which is actually Greek for *I'm keeping secrets from you*," Kimmie says.

"I haven't even told him that I went to Adam's place last night, that the word SOON was written across his bedsheets in some sort of syrupy concoction."

"Corn syrup mixed with red food coloring and cocoa powder." Wes rubs his palms together with enthusiasm. "One of my all-time favorite fake-blood recipes."

"And what, pray tell, did you two do with the sticky evidence?" Kimmie asks me.

I gaze down at my plate of pasta, unable to get the

faux-blood image out of my head. "We put the sheets in his closet."

"Well, you'd best tell Ben about all this," she says. "Otherwise he's apt to accuse you of not giving him the full scoop."

"Funny how he's allowed to keep secrets, while you're practically expected to give hourly updates on the flow, frequency, and color of your urine," Wes says.

"And speaking of secrets and nasty liquids . . ." Kimmie points toward the soda machine.

Ben is there.

And he isn't alone.

There's a flock of senior girls standing around him, including Alejandra Chavez, ranked number one last year on Freetown High School's Most Beautiful People list.

Ben looks at me, and waves, as if he wants to talk.

"So much for taking his lunch period in the library," Kimmie says. "This must be pretty important."

I nod, knowing it probably has something to do with our argument last night. I flag him over, but now it seems he's far too busy talking to Alejandra. She twirls a lock of her inky black hair around her finger and laughs at something he says—so loud we can hear it from ten tables away. Ben peeks over at me again, in midconversation, but still he doesn't move.

"*Awkward*," Kimmie sings. She clears her throat of muffin. "Though, at the risk of sounding like a broken record, I think I might have told you so. I mean, let's face it, supergood looks, a superhero reputation, abs of steel, and a chest that could make a girl weep—"

"His saving your life a bunch of times sort of trumps any of the bad stuff in his past," Wes says, finishing her thought. "At least, that's what people have been saying."

"Ben's a total catch," Kimmie continues.

"And it looks like he's been caught." Wes readjusts the glasses on his face as if that will help him gawk better.

While the other groupies have dispersed, Ben remains talking to Alejandra, like I'm no longer even there.

"It really comes down to one simple question," Kimmie says, reaching out to touch my forearm. "Is helping Adam really worth the cost of what this is doing to your relationship with Ben?"

I push my plate of pasta away and remain focused on Ben, knowing that this is just the beginning, because I need to spend a whole lot more time with Adam if I want to figure things out.

## 35

WHEN I GET OUT OF SCHOOL, Adam is already waiting for me in the parking lot. Ben is waiting, too. He's sitting on his motorcycle, looking in my direction. I'm just about to go talk to him when Freetown High's Most Beautiful Person intercepts my path. Alejandra shows him something inside her coat and then spins around and starts laughing.

Ben is laughing, too, but I can tell it's more of a nervous chuckle, because he gets off his bike and takes a step back.

"Need a ride, little girl?" Wes asks, sneaking up and snatching my attention. "I've got some stale Jujyfruits inside my car."

Tiffany Bunkin is with him. Ironically enough, the front of her T-shirt is decorated with big yellow flowers.

Wes follows my gaze. "Something you want me to sabotage?" He rolls up his sleeves to be funny, as if in fight mode.

"I really think we should get going," Tiffany tells him before I can answer.

Wes checks the time on his digital-camera spy watch. "Agreed. I made reservations for three p.m. sharp at Brain Freeze. What do you say, Chameleon, care to join us for a little frozen sugarized cow cream? The first lick's on me." He winks.

"A tempting offer, but I have work to do."

Wes looks toward Adam's car and then back at Ben and Alejandra, who are still engaged in conversation. "Call me later," he says. "I beg you."

I watch as he and Tiffany take off, which prompts me finally to break things up between Ben and Alejandra.

"Do you have a minute?" I ask him.

Alejandra gives me a dirty look. "We're actually a little busy here." She looks me up and down with her big amber eyes, pausing a moment to grimace at my shoes (for the record, a pair of ugly, aka practical, rubber-soled shoes, worthy of Wes's closet).

"Camelia and I have a lot to talk about," Ben tells her. "But I'll see you tomorrow?"

"Better yet, you can call me tonight." She rips a scrap of paper from her notebook, scribbles down what I presume to be her phone number, hands it to him, and takes off; the heels of her tall leather boots clomp against the pavement with each step.

"Sorry to interrupt," I say, once Alejandra is out of earshot.

"No you're not." He smirks.

"You're right." I smirk back. "I'm not."

Ben takes a step closer and gazes into my eyes, almost making me forget every bit of our drama.

*Almost.*

"Are you still upset with me?" he asks.

"That depends. . . . What's with you and Freetown's MBP?"

"Excuse me?" he asks. His face scrunches up in confusion.

I fold my arms, waiting for the initials to finally click in.

"Oh, you mean Alejandra?" He shrugs like it's no big deal—as if he didn't spend the entire lunch period talking to her today. "Not much. She writes for the school newspaper and wants to do a story on me."

"What kind of story?"

He leans toward me over the seat of his bike. His cheek grazes the side of my face as he whispers into my ear: "Just so you know, some people actually find me newsworthy."

"Very funny, but that's not what I meant."

"Jealous?" he asks, amused by the possibility.

"Hardly," I say, bursting his bubble with a fib.

Ben draws his face away, pausing for a moment to glance at my lips. "Well, that's good, because I'm not really interested in revealing any secrets. I'm a private person, remember? I only let a very select few in."

"But unfortunately that select few doesn't include me," I remind him.

Ben looks away, but he doesn't deny it. "This is just really hard for me."

"It isn't exactly easy for me, either. I'm trying to understand what you won't tell me."

"I'd die if anything bad happened to you." He gazes toward Adam's car.

"Nothing bad will happen to me." I reach out to touch his hand. "Not if you're by my side."

"And what about us?" he asks, taking his hand away. "Can you honestly say the same?"

"Tell me," I insist, "how is helping Adam going to hurt our relationship?"

"It's *already* hurting it." His dark eyes soften as he stares into my face.

"What happened to wanting to help me?" I ask him. "What happened to *we'll work together as a team?* I mean, if the tables were reversed, I'm not so sure I'd like the idea of *you* spending so much time with *my* ex–best friend, someone you used to date. But I'd like to say that I'd understand."

"You don't know what I sensed," he says, sidestepping my questions.

"No," I snap. There's a broken-glass feeling inside my chest. "Because you won't tell me."

"It's complicated."

I take a deep breath, trying to regroup—to hold back the flood of tears that sting my eyes. "Did you sense something that might threaten my life?"

"Do you honestly think I'd let you see Adam at all if I did? I'm not forcing you to stop helping him. I'm asking you."

I shake my head, completely at a loss for what else to say. For what else to do. "Adam was your best friend," I blurt out. "Don't you care if he lives or dies? Don't you care about the guilt I'd have to live with if something bad happened to him because I did nothing to stop it? You of all people know what it's like to live with guilt." I close my eyes, thinking about Aunt Alexia's journal, and am reminded of my mother's guilt as well.

"Yes, but we can hand this whole thing over to the police. It's not like we don't have tangible proof that something weird is going on," Ben says.

"I agree that he should tell the police, but that doesn't mean I can just walk away. The police aren't as connected as I am. They don't sense things the way I do."

"Just think about it," he says, taking his helmet from his handlebars, as if gearing up to go. "That's all I ask."

"And what if I don't? Are you honestly trying to tell me that our relationship will be through?"

"Honestly," his lip quivers; he looks just as lost as I feel. "I don't know."

"I have to go," I say, barely able to hold it all together. I turn on my heel and head for Adam's car.

## 36

*I*T'S QUIET IN THE CAR between Adam and me, which is mostly my fault. While he tries to make me comfortable by cracking corny jokes and asking if there's anything I want to talk about, I remain mostly mute.

A series of turns and over a bridge later, and I notice that we're no longer moving. I look at Adam, wondering what's going on, only to realize that we're parked outside his apartment building.

We've been sitting in front of it for God only knows how long. Meanwhile, I've been stuck in a Ben-filled fog.

We climb the stairs to his floor and enter his apartment. Adam puts on a fresh pot of coffee, bragging about how he once used to work as a barista and therefore knows the importance of grind, water temperature, and foam consistency.

I sit at the kitchen table, pull a stash of crossword

puzzles from my pocket, and try to arrange them in some sort of order, grateful for the distraction, because my insides are absolutely shaking.

"I really appreciate you helping me out with this," he says.

"You don't have to keep thanking me."

"I know." He sets two mugs of coffee on the table. "It's just that it means a lot to me, especially after everything."

I nod, pretty positive he's referring to his shady track record with me.

"Anyway, I'm not so sure I'd do the same if I were in your shoes," he continues.

"Well, you wouldn't let me get hurt," I say, confident that it's the truth.

"No," he says, sitting beside me and holding my gaze for just a moment too long. "I definitely wouldn't."

He smells like mocha, and there's a smudge of coffee grounds on his chin. I'm tempted to tell him about it, but I try to stay focused. I grab a pen and some paper from my bag and make a list of the puzzling messages:

WATCH YOUR BACK
YOU LIED TWO ME
YOU ARE NEVER ALONE. EYE AM ALWAYS WATCHING
EYE WANT TWO SEE YOU BLEED
YOU DESERVE TO DIE
CHECK THE BED
SOON

I read the list over and over again, hoping to make some sense of it. "Have you lied to anyone recently?" I ask him, noticing how one of the Across riddles mentions lying, too.

"I was trying to think about that," he says, "but aside from not being completely honest with you last month . . . no one."

"Well, obviously, this person doesn't agree," I say, remembering how he also lied to me about getting in touch with Tray on the night that someone wrote on his door. "And what about the WATCH YOUR BACK message? It's like somebody's warning you not to trust someone. Do you have any idea who that someone might be?"

Adam shakes his head, clearly at a loss.

"Think hard," I say, "because these are our biggest clues. The other messages are sort of standard stalker stuff."

"I didn't know there was a standard for stalkers."

"It's true." I sigh, nodding toward the list. "Basically, this person is watching you and wants you to know it—a bunch of the Across and Down riddles confirm this, too. This person's telling you who's in control by calling the shots and breaking in to your place. Plus they're mad as hell, as also evidenced by clues like: *You are despicable*; *Sometimes I truly hate you*; *If I cut you, you will bleed.* . . ."

"Wow," he says, seemingly surprised. His face becomes completely solemn. "It sounds so much worse when you put it all together like that."

"This person feels really alone," I continue, referring to several of the other crossword clues. "And there's definitely both a payback component and a timing issue."

"Meaning I did something bad?"

"It's all a matter of perspective," I assure him. "And this person's perspective is obviously skewed. I mean, people in their right mind don't normally send stalker notes, especially ones that you have to decode."

"It doesn't matter." He shakes his head, looking far more serious than I've ever seen him before. "Because, like you said, it's only a matter of time before he or she makes good on all these threats and messages." He taps his finger against the *Opposite of live* clue.

"We'll get through this." I place my hand on his shoulder, noticing that his neck is splotched with hives.

"Thanks," he says, meeting my eyes. "I'm really glad you've been able to forgive me for everything that happened between us."

"It's not such a big deal."

"To me it is."

I look away to inspect the list of messages again, doing my best to keep things focused on the business at hand, but apparently Adam wants to make them personal.

"Can I ask you something?" he says.

I venture to look back up at his face, much against my better judgment.

"I saw you and Ben in the parking lot earlier," he says when I don't answer. "Even before that . . . I saw the way you looked at him when he was talking to that other girl."

"And?" I ask, wondering about the point.

"And I just wonder if he looks at us like that."

I feel my lips part, almost surprised by his perception.

"I just don't want to come between you two," he continues.

"No one's coming between Ben and me," I say, probably a little too quickly.

"Well, that's good." He forces a tiny smile. "Because I know I'm taking your attention from him."

"It's just hard," I admit, noticing that my palms are sweating. There's a streak of perspiration on the table. "Ben and I haven't really gotten a chance to be normal together. There's always been all this other stuff in the way."

"But that's just it. I don't want to *be* all that other stuff."

I bite my lip, thinking how, as horrible as it sounds, and as much as I care for Ben, it would be so much easier to have a boyfriend like Adam.

"Camelia?" he asks, wondering maybe what's on my mind.

I glance at his mouth, reminded of the sculpture I did in pottery class. "Maybe we should see if there's some other way to piece these messages together," I say. I begin to rearrange the puzzles once more.

But Adam stops me by placing his hand over mine. And making my heart pound.

"I really think you should go," he says.

"No," I insist. "We need to solve this thing."

"I actually have a ton of homework to do."

"You're lying."

"Me, lie? Never." He smiles. "Come on, I'll drive you to Ben's."

I'm almost tempted to give him a hug, but instead I grab a napkin and wipe the coffee grounds from his chin.

"Pretty charming, right?"

"Definitely charming," I say, noticing the irresistible curve his grin makes.

And turning away to avoid it.

# AUDIO TRANSCRIPT 9

**DOCTOR:** I've been thinking. I'm not sure how much we're actually accomplishing in these therapy sessions.

**PATIENT:** Does that mean you're giving up on me, too?

**DOCTOR:** Not giving up, just trying to make decisions that are in your best interest.

**PATIENT:** In other words, you suck as a therapist.

**DOCTOR:** I just think that you might have more luck with someone else, or perhaps in a group setting.

**PATIENT:** In other words, *you suck*.

**DOCTOR:** I realize you're upset, but in time you'll see that I'm doing this for you.

**PATIENT:** Where have I heard *that* before?

**DOCTOR:** I don't know. Why don't *you* tell *me*?

**PATIENT:** What for? You're ditching me, remember?

**DOCTOR:** I'll still be in touch. I'll be checking in with your new therapist to see how you're progressing.

**PATIENT:** *(Patient doesn't respond.)*

**DOCTOR:** How does all of this sound to you?

**PATIENT:** *(Still no response.)*

**DOCTOR:** Can you talk to me?

**PATIENT:** I'm done talking. I don't ever want to talk to you again.

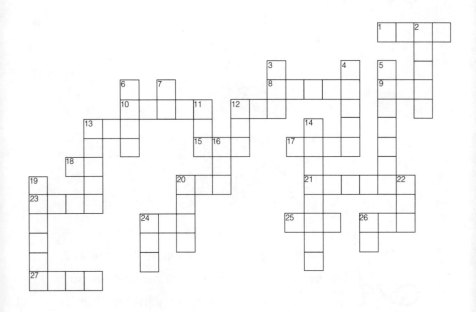

**Across:**

**15.** Not _____ said the cat.

**21.** The library used to own two _____ of the book entitled *Getting What You Want, Regardless of the Cost*, but one of them is permanently mine now.

**Down:**

**6.** You _____ me do it.

## 37

A DAM DROPS ME OFF in front of Ben's house, but unfortunately Ben isn't home, and his aunt doesn't know where he is. I try his cell, but he isn't picking up.

"Do you want to wait for him inside?" his aunt asks, having clearly just gotten off from work. She's still wearing her apron from the florist shop, and her jeans are stained with soil.

I accept because it's freezing out, not to mention that it's started to snow. I call my mom to pick me up, and then sit down at the kitchen table with a mug of his aunt's hot apple cider.

"You and Ben are having problems, aren't you?" she asks, sliding a plate of her homemade sugar cookies at me.

"Did he tell you about them?"

She shakes her head and takes a seat across from me. "But an aunt knows these things," she says, winking.

"We have a keen sense of intuition."

"Really?" I ask, taken aback by her words, because my aunt has a keen sense of intuition, too.

"He's been through a lot, as you know." She tucks a lock of her kinky dark hair behind her ear. "It's made him a bit guarded. He has a hard time letting people get too close."

"Don't I know it." I take a bite of cookie.

"But there's been a change in him in the last couple months," she continues. "And I believe that change is you. Aside from this minor bump in the road, I've never seen him happier." She reaches out to touch my hand. There's a bit of emotion in her eyes.

A second later, my mom beeps the horn out front. I give Ben's aunt a hug, grateful to have her perspective on things, and hoping she's right.

"Hey," Mom says once I get inside her car. A nature CD blares from the radio—the sound of birds chirping, with a waterfall in the background. Mom turns it down and takes us to Raw, claiming to have a hankering for hummus wraps and banana smoothies. Though I sense there's something more.

We take our food and plop down in a booth. "How's Aunt Alexia?" I ask, wondering if Mom's finally willing to talk on the subject.

"She asked about you, too," Mom says. "She was worried that you might be afraid of her after the visit. She feels really bad about her behavior."

"I'm not afraid of her. I want to see her again."

"That's the tricky part. Her therapist doesn't know if she can help her anymore. They've sort of hit a wall in their sessions together, and Aunt Alexia's been referred to someone else."

"I don't understand. She went to Detroit just to work with this therapist. It's barely been a month."

"I know," Mom says, sweeping a clump of curls from in front of her eyes. "But there's someone else who wants to work with her now. It's all very recent, which is why I've been so distracted. Anyway, I'm sorry."

"Don't apologize. Just be honest with me. Tell me what's going on."

"In a nutshell," she begins, gulping down the remainder of her smoothie as if it were a shot of tequila, "what this doctor is proposing sounds kind of controversial, and I'm not sure I agree with it."

"What is he proposing?"

"It's called electroconvulsive therapy."

"Electro . . . as in shock?"

Mom nods again and drinks down my smoothie as well.

"No way," I practically shout. "You can't allow it."

"I haven't agreed to anything."

"Well, *don't*, because it's barbaric. There's nothing wrong with her."

"There *is* something wrong, and this method of treatment is not as barbaric as you might think. Some really cutting-edge doctors still use it. This particular doctor thinks she's a perfect candidate."

"She's not crazy," I insist, pushing my plate away. "Everyone's got it all wrong about her."

"Is there something you're not telling me?" Mom asks. "Did Aunt Alexia say something to you?"

"Just promise me you won't allow this," I say, surprised she'd even entertain such an idea. I study her worried expression and the crackled lines that stretch along the sides of her pursed lips, tempted to finally tell her the truth about me.

But then she nods in agreement, like she knows that shock therapy isn't the answer, either. "I just don't want to fail her," she says, staring down at her plate.

"You won't." I slide my hand across the table and touch her forearm.

Mom smiles at the gesture. "I felt bad keeping you out of the loop. I know you have a genuine interest in your aunt, and I'm proud of you for it."

I take a deep breath, trying to ease the pounding of my heart, the sickly feeling in my gut.

"And before I forget," she continues, wiping her watery eyes, "Aunt Alexia wanted me to tell you something. I'm not sure what she was referring to exactly, but she wanted me to tell you *soon*."

"Soon?" I ask, feeling the hairs stand up on the back of my neck.

"I know; I didn't understand it myself. At first I thought she might have been hoping to see you again soon, because she even asked me to take her home with us. But then she started talking about some boy in her paintings, and how I needed to call the police to try and find him. She was getting more and more incoherent as the conversation progressed, but I thought I'd ask you about it anyway. Do you have any idea what she might have been talking about?"

"No," I lie, knowing for sure now how connected Aunt Alexia and I are, and fully confident that she doesn't belong in a mental hospital.

38

*J*LIE PRETTY LOW in school the following day, heading straight to pottery class in lieu of going to lunch, and bee-lining it for the exit doors as soon as the final bell rings.

I don't see Ben at all. Chemistry class got cut due to someone's lame-o idea of pulling the fire alarm, and I was one of the first people in homeroom this morning, purposely to avoid lingering in the hallways.

Needless to say, I'm pretty disappointed that he didn't call me last night, especially after our argument in the parking lot, and *especially* after I stopped by his house, cutting my time short with Adam.

It's just after dinner, and I'm in my room, tempted to write Aunt Alexia a letter. I grab her journal from beneath my pillow, wondering if I should show a few excerpts to Mom—if reading about the beginning stages of Aunt Alexia's touch powers might help Mom understand her more.

But I'm afraid it might actually make things worse.

Mom would undoubtedly want to read the entire journal, discovering just how miserable Aunt Alexia had truly been growing up—how isolated she'd felt, and how she'd constantly had fantasies of killing herself. Mom would only end up blaming herself even more.

A moment later, someone knocks on my door. I slip the journal under my bedcovers.

"Hey," Dad says, peeking in. He comes and sits on the edge of my bed. He smells like Taco Bell. "I thought you might want to talk. You seemed really upset about Aunt Alexia last night."

"I *was* upset. I still am."

"Anything you want to talk about?"

"I could ask you the same," I say, thinking about Aunt Alexia's journal, and how he didn't even flinch at the sight of it.

Dad removes his glasses. His eyelids seem heavy. His face is flushed. There are heavy, dark circles beneath his eyes. "Your mom told me she filled you in on Aunt Alexia's possible transfer. I suppose I don't need to tell you how upset she is—Mom, I mean. She hasn't been sleeping well at night. She's mostly been staring out our bedroom window, dredging up the past and still blaming herself. A lack of sleep will do that to you."

"What does her therapist say?"

"Talk about therapy not working. I think Mom needs to start seeing someone new."

"What can I do?" I ask.

"Just be patient with her, okay? Help her out. Let her know where you're going. Eat her healthy cooking without squawking too much." He smiles. "And don't do anything stupid."

"In other words, no stress."

"No stress." He winks. "I just don't think she'd be able to handle it right now."

"How are you handling it?" I ask, thinking about all the problems that developed between them after Aunt Alexia's suicide attempt this past fall.

"Fine," he says, looking away, as if maybe he has secrets, too.

"Are you sure?"

He nods and takes my hand, able to hear the concern in my voice. "I love your mother more than anything," he says, and then kisses my forehead. He offers to talk some more, but his eyes get heavier by the moment, no doubt because he's been staying awake at night with Mom.

I tell him I need to finish my homework, and then, once he leaves, I grab the phone to call Ben.

"Hey," he says, picking up on the first ring. "My aunt said that you stopped by yesterday."

"Yeah," I say. "Where were you?"

"Nowhere important. Just riding around."

I look out my window at the snow-covered branches. "Even though it was twenty degrees out and snowing?"

"Where were *you*?" he asks, ignoring the question.

"You *know* where. You saw me drive away with Adam."

There's silence between us for several seconds except

for the sound of each other's breath.

"I just thought you would've called me," I say, disappointed that I even have to mention it, that he doesn't bring it up himself, and that once again he's being so closed off—not asking me how I am, or what Adam and I talked about, or even what I've been doing all day.

"I know," he says, finally. "I definitely should have."

"So, why didn't you?"

More silence, only this time it's even louder. And the pain in my chest burrows deeper.

"Is it because I was with Adam?" I ask.

"I'm not jealous if that's what you're thinking."

I bite my lip, thinking how distant he sounds, like this whole conversation is just a big waste of time for him. "Why not?" I ask; the words shoot out of my mouth before my brain has the time to stop them.

"I don't know. Why would I be?"

I shake my head, disappointed by his response, because maybe in some small and selfish way I *want* him to be jealous. I want him to be superinquisitive as to what Adam and I have been up to—to check up on me throughout the day and be the last person I speak to at night.

"Camelia?"

"Are you going to tell me what you've been sensing?" I ask, giving him one final opportunity to let me in.

"I really don't think—"

"Forget it," I say, cutting him off. I tell him that I have to go and hang up before he has a chance to say good-bye.

## 39

*J* SIT PERCHED ON MY BED, confused about what just happened. I gaze out the window again, catching my reflection in the glass. My image is a blurry haze, muddied by the tears that drip down the sides of my face. Still, I tell myself that, as bad as this feels, and as much as it stings, I'm doing the right thing by helping Adam.

I just wish Ben thought so, too.

A few moments later, my cell phone rings. I hold myself back from answering right away, wondering if it's him, if he's calling to say that he made a giant mistake. I check the caller ID only to discover that it isn't Ben at all.

It's Kimmie.

"Hello?" she asks, when I pick up and don't say anything. "Camelia, are you there?"

"I'm here," I mumble.

"What's going on? You barely said two words in

sculpture class, and then you didn't even show up at lunch. . . ."

"I can't really talk right now."

"Is it because I didn't call you last night? I was going to, but I got so wrapped up in Nate's stupid science project. By the way, did you know that not only do Twinkies double in size when submerged in water but they also turn brown after twenty-four hours?"

"I can't really talk right now," I repeat. My voice is as broken as I feel.

"What's wrong?" she asks. "You're freaking me out."

"I have to go. I'll call you later?" Without waiting for her answer, I flip the phone shut and turn it off completely. I take the home phone off the hook as well.

Lying back in bed, I pull the covers over me, still able to smell Ben in my sheets.

About twenty minutes later, Mom knocks on my bedroom door.

"I've got it from here," Kimmie says to my mother, opening the door wide. "Camelia, I'm so glad you're home. I'm having some serious parental problems that only you would understand."

I sit up in bed, noticing how she looks like the Swiss Miss cocoa girl, with her corseted top and apron skirt. She closes the door behind her, and then joins me on my bed, allowing me to collapse into her arms. She strokes my hair, offers me tissues, and reminds me that everything will be okay.

"Whatever this is, you'll get through it," she tells me.

I nod, knowing she's right, because I trust Kimmie. I trust her with my life. Obviously Ben can't say the same about me.

# 40

I T'S STILL A LITTLE WHILE before I'm able to talk to Kimmie about stuff. I tell her about what happened after school with Adam yesterday, as well as about my most recent phone conversation with Ben.

"So, where does this leave you and Ben?" she asks.

"I don't know," I say; the words burn in my throat. I grab a pillow and hug it to my stomach. Meanwhile, Kimmie continues to try and soothe me by running her fingers through my hair and patting my back.

"Well, you have to admit, it was sort of sweet of Adam to drop you off at Ben's house, especially if he really *is* wigged out about what's been happening with the notes and stuff."

"I know," I say, reminded that I should call him tonight.

"So, any theories as to what Ben might be sensing?"

"Not really, but it's all I've been thinking about."

"Well, if it's supposed to protect your relationship, then it has to be something involving the two of you."

"I guess," I say, still unclear as to why that means I should stop helping Adam.

"So, what are you going to do?" she asks, giving me a pointed look—literally. There's an arrow-shaped barbell ring piercing her eyebrow.

"What else? I'm going to continue trying to help Adam."

"Good answer."

"I thought you said I should back off."

"I did, but that wouldn't be like you, which is precisely the reason I allow you to be my best friend."

"So, then, let me *be* a best friend," I say. "Tell me about your recent bout of parental problems."

"Huh?" She makes a face. Her black false eyelashes curl up toward the ceiling. "Oh, you mean that stuff I blabbed on my way in here? That was just something I made up to get past your goalie of a mother."

"You're my best friend, too," I say, giving her a hug, knowing that she could undoubtedly talk for hours on end about the issues she has with her parents, but that she wants to be here for me instead.

A FTER KIMMIE LEAVES, I click my phone back on and give Adam a call.

"I've been thinking about you all day," he says. "I was going to call you last night, but I got busy at work. Anyway, I feel bad about causing problems between you and Ben."

"Except you're not the one causing them."

"Are you sure? Because, just say the word and I'll make myself extinct," he says. "I'll be a pale and distant memory in your otherwise colorful life."

"We probably shouldn't be talking about your extinction anytime soon."

"Then what should we be talking about?" he asks.

"How about getting together tonight? We can pick up where we left off yesterday afternoon."

"Can it wait until tomorrow?"

"Are you busy?" I ask, eager for the distraction.

"It's just that Piper's here. We're making some midnight snacks."

"Three hours early," I hear her shout in the background, then she lets out a giggly little laugh.

"I'm sorry," I say, feeling suddenly self-conscious. "I'll call you tomorrow."

"No, wait," he says, before pressing the mute button so I can't hear him. He comes back on the line a few seconds later, saying he'll come and pick me up.

"Adam—no. I don't want to ruin your plans."

"It's no big deal. Piper's actually just leaving."

"Are you sure?" I ask, feeling worse by the minute, especially since Piper sounded so chipper just moments ago, as if leaving were the last thing on her mind.

"Don't worry, she didn't go empty-handed. She took a whole bowl of cinnamon pretzels with her. So, I'll come and get you?"

I reluctantly agree and grab my coat, slip on my shoes, and climb out the window. Adam meets me at the corner of my street, and we drive around for at least a half hour discussing the details of the messages and crossword puzzles.

"How have things been with Tray?" I ask.

Adam shrugs and turns up the heat to stifle the chill. "He reminded me that his apartment was broken into earlier this year. The door locks in our apartment building are sort of a joke. And so is all the drama. But at least he and I are talking again."

"How about your old roommate? Does he still have a key?"

"No. He gave me his set when he moved out."

"So, you didn't change the lock?"

"What for?"

"Do you think he has a copy somewhere? Did you guys end things on good terms?"

"If you call his adding green food coloring to my shampoo, jock itch cream to my aftershave, and ground Ex-Lax to my coffee grinds 'good terms' . . . then, yes."

I shake my head, noticing the bacon-scented air freshener that dangles from his rearview mirror. "More drama, I take it."

"But not enough drama to wish me dead. It was lame-o girlfriend stuff," he explains. "Like with Tray. Basically, I couldn't stand that his girlfriend practically lived at our place but didn't pay any rent."

"I just don't get it with Tray," I tell him. "I mean, you didn't even know he was interested in Melissa when you asked her out."

"I'd like to say I didn't, but who knows? Maybe part of me did. Maybe part of me likes the idea of hooking up with people who are already spoken for."

"Like what happened with Julie?" I ask, taking the bait.

"And with you," he says. "I mean, maybe if you and Ben weren't together, you wouldn't be half as appealing to me."

"Really?" I ask, surprised by his honesty.

"Not really," he says; his face is completely serious.

He pulls into the parking lot of an all-night diner,

puts the car in park, and then turns to me, studying my face, waiting for a reaction.

But I have no idea what to say.

Heat blasts in through the dashboard vents, warming my cheeks.

"Are you hungry?" he asks, nodding toward the entrance.

I shake my head, thinking how it wasn't so long ago that Ben and I came here on a night like this—on a night when I'd snuck out my bedroom window just to be with him.

"So, I guess we really don't have any other choice but to wait and see what happens," he says.

"Unless you want to go to the police."

"I told you why I don't."

"Because you think Ben's the one doing this?"

"That's one reason." He swallows hard. "And I'm not exactly sure it's true, but I'm not willing to take that chance, either."

"Meaning?"

"Maybe I was too quick to blame him for Julie's death. Maybe I'm partially to blame as well."

"That's quite a turnaround from trying to take revenge."

"What can I say? I've talked to some people about it."

"What people?"

"It doesn't really matter." His eyes remain locked on mine. "What matters is that I shouldn't have been seeing his girlfriend in the first place. Maybe if I'd been honest with him he wouldn't have freaked out on the trail that day when she told him the truth."

"But hindsight is twenty-twenty, right?"

"I just don't want to cause him more grief—even if he is the one doing all this."

"And if he isn't—which I know is the truth?"

Adam shakes his head and sits back in his seat. "What are the odds that this'll all blow over?"

"You're asking the wrong person."

"Yeah." He laughs. "I guess I am."

"You want a little advice?"

"Besides going to the police?"

"Talk to Ben. Tell him what you told me . . . about Julie."

Adam turns to me again. The light from the diner sign shines across his face, illuminating his deep brown eyes. "You really think so?"

"Yeah. I mean, I think he'd really want to hear it. I think he really *deserves* to hear it."

"I know. It's just—it's sort of a lot to admit."

I gaze at his mouth, reminded of its shape—the way his top lip is slightly fuller than the bottom, the way his mouth turns upward at the corners even though he's no longer smiling—and the scar that runs along his bottom lip.

"Camelia?" he asks, noticing maybe that I can't stop staring. "We should probably get going, don't you think?"

"Yeah," I say, but I don't move an inch.

Music plays from his stereo; it's a singer with a

soulful, sultry voice who aches for second chances. And makes me ache, too. Ironically, it's the same song that played in Adam's car that night three weeks ago—in front of my house at the end of our date, when I knew he wanted to kiss me.

"Camelia?" he repeats; I can feel his breath on my cheek. He touches the side of my face, perhaps silently asking for my permission.

I tell myself that this is wrong, and that I should back away.

But I don't.

A few moments later, I feel his lips press against mine. He tastes like peppermint candy, which prompts me to kiss him longer, deeper.

Until the kiss breaks.

And I finally come to my senses.

# 42

ON THE DRIVE HOME, Adam glances at me several times, clearly wanting to talk about what's happened.

But I can barely look up from the door latch.

Exactly six pain-filled minutes later, he pulls over at the corner of my street and puts the car in park. "Do you hate me?" he asks.

"More like I hate myself."

"Yeah." He sighs. "Kissing me tends to have that effect on women."

"That's not what I meant."

"Don't worry about it," he says, still trying to make light of the situation. "It's my fault. It won't happen again."

"I *let* it happen."

"Yes, but only because you couldn't help yourself. I must admit, I'm far too irresistible for my own good."

"I wouldn't go that far." I can't help but smile.

"Don't worry about it," he says again. "I know you didn't mean it."

I manage to look up at him finally, noticing that his eyes are tired and red. "Did *you* mean it?"

Instead of answering, Adam pushes a lock of hair from in front of my face, making my heart stir. "No one besides us has to know about tonight, okay?"

I nod, almost wishing that he weren't so understanding about things. "I think I'm just feeling really vulnerable tonight," I say, as though an explanation would make it all better—provide a rational excuse for what felt so instinctive. "I had an argument with Ben, and you were being so open and honest with me about everything. I felt really close to you."

"Well, I'm flattered," he says, moving back behind the wheel. "And I'm sorry that it happened at all."

I feel my chin quiver at his words, wondering if he really believes them. We say our good nights, and I head up the street to my house. I crawl inside my window, tempted to give Kimmie a call to tell her the whole story, but for now I just want to be by myself. So that no one can tell me that what I did was wrong. Because in Adam's car, with the heat blasting over us, it just felt horribly and inexcusably right.

I ARRANGE TO MEET Kimmie and Wes before homeroom the following day. The cafeteria serves breakfast for early risers in the form of stale toast, oatmeal sludge, and watered-down orange juice.

"This had better be worth it," Wes says. "By my calculations, I'd say you're denying us at least thirty minutes of sleep."

"Not to mention precious primping time." Kimmie motions to her outfit: a black leather poodle skirt paired with a glittery pink T that reads DEMON IN TRAINING. "Like it? I also have a coordinating pitchfork, but in all this rush I forgot it at home."

"Along with your sense of style," Wes jokes, resting his cheek against her shoulder.

"So, are we to assume that this impromptu meeting has something to do with Ben?" she asks.

I nod and tell them about the kiss.

"Okay, so this was *definitely* worth the dark circles under my eyes," Kimmie says. "Details, please. How was it?"

"No details. It just sort of happened. The kiss itself was . . . fine."

Kimmie glares at me, her mouth hanging open like I'm full-on crazy. "'Fine'? You had his *tongue* in your mouth. I demand a description."

"Was it sloppy, too dry, or with just the right amount of spittle?" Wes asks.

"Did your teeth avoid clanking? Did your tongues swirl in sync? Did he have fresh-smelling breath?" Kimmie adds.

"It was good," I say, eager to move on. My face heats up as I replay the moment of the kiss in my mind.

Kimmie sighs at my lack of details. "Well, I must say, I'm not so surprised it happened, especially considering all the Ben drama. Last I talked to you, you didn't even know if you two were still together."

"Right, it's called rebound," Wes says, like I need the explanation. "And it can be damned tasty in the right situation." He takes an enthusiastic bite of toast.

"Do you think kissing Adam had anything to do with the sculpture you did of his pouty mouth?" She puckers, too. "Like, maybe the sculpture was a premonition. . . ."

"And what other body parts will you be sculpting and acting upon in the near future?" Wes asks. "I've got a really interesting—"

"Thank you *very* much." I cut him off.

"You're not going to tell Ben about this, are you?" he asks. "Because it's not like he's been telling *you* anything."

"Except he'll probably be able to sense it anyway," Kimmie reminds him.

"Telling him is the right thing to do," I say. "It's just going to kill him. I mean, in his eyes, this will be the second time Adam's taken someone away from him. It's no wonder he has trust issues."

"Don't be so hard on yourself," Wes says. "You're primal in nature and thus bound to fall prey to your own beastly instincts, which is exactly what I told Tiffany Bunkin on our date last night. That girl can't keep her hands off me."

"A good thing?" I ask him.

Wes shrugs and drinks Kimmie's juice down to the pulp. "I mean, she's cute and all—in a wildflower sort of way—but I'm not so sure she does it for me."

"Because you're far more interested in weeds?" Kimmie asks.

"I'm giving her another chance," he says, ignoring the question. "We're going out tomorrow night."

"Just like my parents," Kimmie says. "I've got it all set up. Nate has a sleepover at his friend's house, and I've made a reservation for three at Cuvée. I'm telling my parents I need to meet them there, because I'm helping you with math homework"—she winks at me—"I'll give them a few minutes to themselves and then call the host and have him tell them I'm not feeling well and can't make it out."

"Very original." Wes rolls his eyes. "Did I not see that same scene in the movie *Parent Trap* when I was seven?"

"It happened in the last season of *Totally Teen Princess*, if you must know," Kimmie says. "And it totally worked. Frannie's parents got back together."

"And so you know the plan is foolproof," Wes jokes.

"Be sure to tell us how it goes," I say, praying she doesn't get her hopes up, though fairly certain they're already pretty high.

I N CHEMISTRY, I DON'T tell Ben about what happened with Adam. Nor do I tell him after school, when I spot him in the parking lot. But by Saturday morning, when he calls and tells me that he wants to talk, I'm determined to come clean.

I open the front door to let him in. "Hey," I say, noticing right away how amazing he looks. There's a trace of stubble on his face, like he's just gotten out of bed, and his hair is rumpled from his helmet.

"I got us some bagels." He holds up the bag.

"Thanks," I say, taking his coat and leading him into the kitchen. I set a couple of plates down on the island. "I hope herbal tea is okay. My mother has this weird thing about caffeine."

"Sure." He smiles. "Tea would be great."

I heat up the kettle, pour us a couple of mugs, and then sit on a stool opposite him. I force down a bite of bagel, even though I have no appetite. In my mind I try to formulate the gentlest way to tell him.

"I'm really sorry about everything that's been happening between us," Ben says before I can start. "I haven't really been fair."

I bite my lip to stop the trembling, feeling horrible that he's the one apologizing. "It just seems like you keep pushing me away. We get so close, but then you won't let me in."

"I want to let you in now. I want to tell you everything." Ben stares at me, seemingly eager for a response.

"What's with the big turnaround?" I ask, looking down at my plate.

"You have to understand what it's been like for me. I've spent so much time on my own these past few years. I thought that maybe I could do it again, that maybe all this stuff I've been feeling—this anxiety, I mean—hasn't been worth it. But it *is* worth it." He leans in closer, forcing me to look at him again. "Because I honestly can't live without you in my life."

My heart swells and then breaks again. I want so much to return the sentiment, but I can barely even speak.

"As much as I hate to admit it," he continues, "I kind of like that you want to help Adam, that you're so willing to do the right thing despite the consequences. And you're right, I do know about living with guilt. I don't want you to have to live with it, too."

"I may have no other choice."

"We'll figure this out. Just look at what happened

the last time we combined forces."

"I know," I say, thinking about the sculpture we did together, and feeling my whole body start to shake.

"Camelia?" he says, clearly noticing how jittery I feel. He reaches out to touch my hand, but I pull away before he can.

"What's the secretive thing you've been sensing?" I ask. "The thing that supposedly might jeopardize our relationship . . ."

"I'm sorry about that, too. It was stupid not to tell you."

"So, tell me now," I say, though suddenly reluctant to know the truth.

"I sensed it first in gym," he begins, "when you showed up and surprised me . . . when I got knocked down . . ."

"After sculpture class."

He nods. "And then I sensed it off and on whenever I'd touch you. The thing is, I know it couldn't happen. I know you'd never do anything to hurt me. I trust you. Completely."

A storm of tears rages behind my eyes, because I know now what he sensed. I press my eyes shut and keep my hands in my lap under the table, where he can't possibly touch them.

And know how ashamed I feel.

"I sensed that you and Adam kissed." His face flashes red. "I know it's completely stupid. I know it would never happen, that you'd never do anything like that. I trust you," he says again. "So, don't hate me, okay?"

"I could never hate you," I mutter, faking a sip of tea to cover my expression.

I know I should tell him the truth. I *want* to tell him the truth. But my voice is broken. My head's all woozy. And my insides feel like they're bleeding.

My parents come in a couple of seconds later. Dad prattles on about how Mom forced him to take a yoga class this morning. Mom lectures us on the evils of the hormone-infested cream cheese on our gluten-containing bagels.

Meanwhile, Ben excuses himself, saying that he promised his aunt he'd help her unload some bags of topsoil at her flower shop. "I'll call you later?" he says, getting up from the stool.

I manage a nod and watch him leave, but I don't walk him to the door. Or even give him a hug good-bye.

## 45

*B* Y LATE AFTERNOON, I'm still reeling. I don't even have the nerve to call Kimmie. It's not that I think she'd lecture me. It's just that I'm not particularly proud of myself right now, and I'm not quite ready to share that.

At about six o'clock, my phone rings. I flip it open, assuming it's Ben, readying myself to tell him that we have much more to talk about.

But it's Adam. "Hey," he says, "are you busy?"

"Why?" I ask, detecting a hint of alarm in his voice.

"We need to talk. I'm actually only a block away from your house. Could I borrow you for a little bit?"

"Sure," I say, wondering why Ben hasn't called like he said he would, and hoping this doesn't take too long.

We hang up, and I tell my parents that I shouldn't be more than an hour. A couple of minutes later, Adam picks me up, and we take off right away.

"Where are we going?" I ask, noticing how unusually quiet he's being, and how he seems to have a definite mission in mind.

"I need to show you something," he says, stepping on the accelerator and shifting into high gear.

We race down a bunch of streets, but eventually it appears we're headed for his apartment. Adam pulls into a parking space in the back lot and switches off his ignition.

"What's going on?" I demand.

"I locked my door," he whispers. "I'm almost sure I did."

"What are you talking about?"

"I tried to call other people," he says, staring down at his steering wheel. "But Tray and Janet took a bus ride to one of her competitions, and I have no idea where Melissa and Piper are."

"Adam," I say, touching his forearm, trying to snag his attention, "you're not making any sense."

"I have something to show you," he says again. He looks up at me finally. His eyes are red, as if he hasn't slept.

"Let's go," I say, finally taking charge. I open the door and step outside. A chill in the air bites at my neck. Meanwhile, two of the main parking-lot lights have been broken. Glass lies shattered against the pavement.

I click on my key-chain flashlight (a stocking stuffer Dad bought me) and lead us through the side entrance, trying to imagine what the urgency is. Did Adam find another crossword puzzle? Could the message possibly be even more disturbing than what we've already seen? Is he even being genuine?

Just before opening the door that leads to his floor, I grab my cell phone and check for a signal. It lights up right away, but then goes dead, as if the battery's out.

"Are you planning to call someone?" he asks.

"No." I flip my phone shut, hoping he didn't see that it isn't working. I begin down the hallway that leads to his apartment, reminded once again of the *YOU DESERVE TO DIE* message written across his door, and of how Adam chose to erase it before anyone could see it.

"There it is," Adam says, nodding toward his door. It takes me a second to spot it: the navy blue scarf tied around the knob.

"Is that yours?" I ask, pretty positive that I've seen him wearing it.

"Yeah," he says. "But it was in my closet, inside my apartment. I know it was."

"Meaning, someone went into your apartment, took it from your closet, and tied it to the knob for no apparent reason?"

"I know," he says, standing uncomfortably close to me now. "It sounds crazy."

"Not crazy, just not fully thought out. Maybe someone borrowed the scarf without telling you, and now they're returning it."

"No one borrowed it."

"That you know of," I counter, thinking that it wouldn't be such a stretch, considering how people seem to borrow his apartment whenever they feel like it. "Or, maybe you were wearing the scarf and accidentally left it out someplace. Maybe someone recognized that it was yours and left it here for you."

"I don't know," he says. "I mean, I don't think so."

"Is the door locked now?" I ask, noticing how quiet it is on the floor.

"No. That's the weird part. I could've sworn I locked it."

I take a deep breath, remembering that he mentioned before how easy it was to break in to these apartments. "So, have you gone in to check things out?"

"I probably should have, but I wanted someone here with me first—a witness—because I almost feel like I'm going crazy."

I nod, knowing exactly what he means.

Adam opens the door and turns on some lights. At first, things appear pretty normal, but then I enter the kitchen and see his dry-erase board.

The photo is the first thing I notice. There's a snapshot of Adam pasted to the board.

"What the hell is that?" he asks, taking a couple steps closer.

It's a picture of him playing basketball in a gym. Someone's drawn on the photo, adding a noose around his neck. There are letter spaces below the image, where someone's filled in the words *I HOPE YOU ARE ENJOYING MY DEADLY LITTLE GAME*, all in capital letters.

"We should go." He shakes his head and runs his

fingers through his hair in frustration. "I need to take you home."

"No," I say, grabbing his arm. "We need to figure this out. When was this photo taken?"

"I don't know. I hit the gym a couple nights a week to shoot hoops. I've been doing it since I moved here."

"Alone?"

"Not usually. Sometimes I go with Tray, sometimes my old roommate's there and decides to join in. Piper's been known to come along on occasion; so have Melissa and Janet. Some nights, if we're up late studying and need to keep ourselves awake, we'll go shoot for a half hour or so."

"Which gym?" I ask, still trying to make sense of things.

"The one at school."

"Who's allowed to access it?"

"Just students, in theory, but it's not exactly Fort Knox. Anyone could borrow a student ID and get in."

"Yes, but who would go to all that trouble?"

"Maybe Wes," he says, checking for my response.

"Wes?"

"Why not? Did you not see the hangman game he drew on here . . . when he called me an idiot?"

"You're not serious," I say, raising my voice.

"Well, I'm not ruling him out."

"I think we definitely need to call the police," I say, refusing to entertain his Wes theory for even one solitary second.

"And what will we say? That I leave my door unlocked on occasion and my friends take advantage of it? That somebody potentially borrowed my scarf without telling me?"

"Let's talk about this," I say, hoping to convince him.

"Let's get you home," he says instead. He opens his door to lead me out.

For once, I decide not to argue, even though I probably should.

# 46

ONCE WE'RE BACK INSIDE Adam's car, he starts the ignition and a rap song blares out—so loud that I have to cover my ears.

"What's the—" he says, fumbling with the dial to turn it down. "Did you change my radio station?"

At the same moment, an alarm clock goes off somewhere in the car. It's a monotonous ping that bullets through my heart. Adam switches on the overhead light, and we both turn to see where the noise is coming from.

There's something on the backseat. A dark blanket covers a mound of some sort.

"What's that?" I ask him.

Adam shakes his head and reaches for the blanket. In one quick motion, he whisks it away.

A doll sits beneath it, wearing a ruffled white suit. It's a clown doll with happy red lips, bright orange hair, and a stark white face. Marionette strings hang loose from its arms, legs, and mouth, and two bloodred tears run from its eyes. The doll holds a large manila envelope that reads, LOOK AT ME. In its other hand is a plastic knife with splotches of fake blood on the handle and blade. A sticky note on the clown's belly reads, PLAY ME.

Meanwhile, the alarm clock continues to flash and chime, signaling that it's five o'clock—even though it's well past six.

Adam takes the clock and turns it off. "What the hell is all this?"

I lean over to pull the sticky note away, then lift up the clown's shirt, wondering if there's a button somewhere that makes the clown talk. Why else would the note say, PLAY ME?

"What are you doing?" Adam asks.

"Following directions," I say, finally finding the button. I push it and a high-pitched giggly voice squeaks: *"See my strings? Well, I pull yours. I follow you. And unlock your doors. I'm watching you, and that's no lie, and very soon, someone's gonna die. Make no mistake, this game's no fake, 'cause I'll see you at our sad little wake. Our time will come, when the clock bells chime, and at that time you will be mine."*

"When the clock bells chime?" Adam asks, looking back at the alarm clock.

"But it's already after five."

"So, maybe we missed something?"

I reach for the manila envelope, noticing that someone's drawn our favorite crossword puzzle on the back.

Adam takes it and reads off the clues. As usual, the answers are pretty obvious.

*"EYE MADE COPIES,"* Adam says, reading the message aloud.

"Open it," I say, already sensing the worst.

With fumbling fingers he tears the seal and peeks inside. His eyes snap shut at what he's seen.

"What is it?" I ask. There's an acid taste inside my mouth.

Adam pulls a sheet of paper from the envelope and turns it over so I can see. It's a snapshot of Adam and me in his car last night. Kissing.

**47**

I TELL ADAM TO GO to the police, and then I bolt from his Bronco and race down the street.

He tries to stop me, shouting out my name and making an effort to follow me in his car. But I cut across a grassy field, not really giving him much of a chance.

I just really need to see Ben right now.

I get to a bus stop about three minutes later. *"I made copies,"* I whisper, anxious to know if Ben's already seen the photo. Maybe that's why he hasn't called.

I take the Number 6 bus to the end of Ben's street. His motorcycle is parked in the driveway. My heart pounds as I climb the front steps.

Ben comes to the door as soon as I ring the bell. "Hey," he says, motioning me in. "I've been trying to call you, but your phone isn't working."

"Oh, right," I say, remembering my uncharged cell.

"Are you okay?" He tries to look into my face.

But I can barely peek up from the rug.

"What's wrong?" he asks.

"Just hold me," I say, collapsing against his chest, half hoping he can sense the truth on his own—that I won't have to say the words.

Ben strokes my hair and holds me close. He smells like topsoil and roses—like the inside of his aunt's flower shop. I breathe him in and glance over his shoulder.

And that's when I see it.

A manila envelope, just like the one in Adam's car.

It sits on the coffee table, along with a bunch of other mail. Ben's name is scribbled across the front in thick black marker.

I take a step back, breaking our embrace.

"What's wrong?" he asks again, following my gaze.

I try to distract him by saying that I need some water, that I'm chilled, that I'd like him to get me a sweater from his room.

"Are you not feeling well?" he asks, seemingly unfazed by the envelope.

"No," I say, knowing that I'd absolutely die if he saw the photo, especially before I had the opportunity to tell him about it.

"We need to talk," I say. "But not here. Can we go somewhere . . . on your bike?"

"Sure," he says, then heads into the family room to get his jacket. Meanwhile, I grab the envelope from the table and hurry to stuff it inside the waistband of my pants.

I start to zip my jacket over it, but the envelope falls out when I take a step.

I pick it up and cram it inside the back of my pants. Ben catches me.

He stands in the kitchen doorway with a bottle of water in his hand. "You said you were thirsty."

My head starts spinning and nerves collide in my chest. I truly feel like I'm going to be sick.

"What's that?" he asks.

I half shrug and take the envelope out. Ben comes and hands me the water bottle. He tries to pry the envelope from my grip, finally spotting his name written across it.

Not knowing what else to do, I keep a firm hold on the edge of the envelope.

"What are you doing?" His brow is furrowed, as if he doesn't quite get why I'm acting so weird—as if he thinks that maybe I'm confused.

I try to rip the envelope out of his hand completely, but it's as if he already senses something from it. His grip tightens, and he yanks it away, accidentally cutting my hand on the edge. Blood seeps from my palm.

"Ben, no," I say, ignoring the cut. "Let's just go somewhere to talk."

Ben shakes his head and starts to tear the envelope open.

"No!" I shriek, lunging for it again. I grasp at air as he turns from me. And takes the photo out.

"I'm sorry!" I shout. Tears stream down my cheeks. "Please hear me out!"

Ben stumbles backward at what he sees. He runs his fingers over the date printed in the corner. "Yesterday," he whispers. "This happened yesterday."

"Please," I repeat. My chest heaves as I gasp for breath.

"Just go," he says, raising his voice.

"I can't," I say. "Not until you talk to me, until you hear what I have to say."

Ben grabs his keys and heads for the door, pulling away when I try to hold him back. He hops on his bike and takes off down the street, leaving me standing on the front steps.

"No!" I shout. My voice fills with more tears. I collapse to the ground, as if I've been stabbed in the gut.

A few moments later, the sky opens up. Freezing rain pours down over me, soaking my skin, making it feel like every inch of me is crying.

## 48

*J*REMAIN ON BEN'S STEPS, figuring he'll come back—that since he's on his bike, he'll be anxious to seek shelter, change out of his wet clothes, get off the slick streets.

But he doesn't come home.

After about an hour of waiting, I go to the phone booth at the end of the street, ready to call Kimmie. But then I remember her plans for tonight—the scheme to set up her parents at the restaurant. Wes is busy, too—out on a date with Tiffany.

Not knowing where else to go and unable to face my parents' inquisitive stares, I give them a quick call, telling them I'm with Wes. And then I head to Knead, where I know I can be alone. It's Saturday night, and Spencer usually leaves after the four o'clock wheel class.

I push my key into the lock and flick on the studio lights.

But Spencer is here, after all. He stands at the back, just outside his office. "What happened?" he asks.

My eyes burn from the pelting rain and the salt of my tears. "It's raining," I say, as if it weren't completely obvious.

"And so you decided to lay out in it?"

"Not exactly," I whisper, stifling a cough. Water drips down the sides of my face.

"What happened?" he asks, peeling off his sweatshirt. He comes and wraps it around me, and then looks into my face.

"What are you doing here?" I ask, trying to distract him from how broken I must look.

"I could ask you the same."

Rain drips from the ends of my hair, landing on the front of his T-shirt. I move to one of the worktables, trying to be tough—to act like I'm just here to sculpt.

"You're soaking wet," Spencer says. "Let me get you some dry clothes. I think I have an old pair of jeans in my office."

"Thanks, but I have my own clothes." I head for the coatroom downstairs, where I keep an extra pair of sweats and sneakers for glazing disasters. I wrench the rain-soaked clothes from my body and wring them out in the sink, feeling my skin turn to gooseflesh. Still, there's a numbness inside me. Because nothing could hurt as much as seeing Ben's face when he opened that envelope.

And knowing how much I hurt him.

I change into dry clothes, including Spencer's sweatshirt, and remain in the bathroom for way longer than I should. Spencer calls out to me at least three times, asking if I'm okay, but I don't have the words to answer.

Finally, he knocks on the door, prompting me to pick myself up off the concrete floor and make my way back upstairs.

"Can we talk?" he asks.

"Not now," I say, pushing past him into the studio area. I try taking the twist tie off a bag of clay; the cut on my hand stings.

"Who do you think you're talking to?" he persists.

I shake my head, still fumbling with the twist tie, doing my best to stay in control, to make things normal, despite how truly abnormal everything feels.

Spencer can see it, too. He pulls the bag of clay from me, forcing me to look at him. "What happened?" he asks again.

"I screwed up," I whisper, allowing him to wrap his arms around me.

He calls Svetlana to tell her he's going to be late for their date tonight, and then he sits me down in his office, bandages my hand, and assures me that everything will work out.

I end up telling him about what happened between Adam and me: the kiss, and how someone must have been spying on us, because they sent a photo of said kiss to Ben.

"Who would spy on you?" he asks.

"I don't know," I say, thinking about Melissa. "I mean, there's this girl who's been majorly crushing on Adam—"

"Ever think it might've been Ben himself?"

"Now you sound like Adam."

"It's possible," he says, sitting beside me on the couch. His straggly dark hair is almost as long as mine now. "At the very least, it's definitely someone who wants to piss you off."

"And break Ben and me up."

"Or break you and Adam up," he suggests.

"Even though we're not together."

"Obviously, this person doesn't believe that," he says, tucking a strand of my wet hair behind my ear. "And how about you? Do you believe it?"

I swallow hard, taken aback by the question, because up until now I've been so worried about everything else— about what Ben might be feeling, about what Ben isn't telling me, what Adam's intentions are, and whether or not I'm doing everything right—that I haven't really asked myself what it is that *I'm* feeling.

Spencer places his hand on mine in an effort to soothe me. His arms are cut up from all his work with various metals—all the chiseling and carving he does. "You'll figure things out. You're an artist, after all. You need to experience life with all its wonders and agonies if you want to produce anything meaningful. Suffering makes you stronger, right?"

"I guess," I say, forcing a tiny smile.

"And now you should go sculpt something really *great*."

I let out a sigh, knowing he's right.

While Spencer gathers his stuff to leave, I manage to

get the tie off the bag of clay and wire off a nice thick slab. I wedge out my clay, despite my bandage, eager to try to avoid my Ben thoughts with clues concerning the crossword puzzles and messages. I close my eyes and the image of the knife from my aunt's painting pops into my head. And so I sculpt it, adding Ben's initials—B.C.—to the surface of the knife's blade without thinking.

I open my eyes, suddenly realizing what I've done, knowing that I have to get him out of my head if I want to remain focused and figure things out once and for all. I wipe my hands on an apron and grab the studio phone to call Adam.

"Hey," he says, picking up right away. "I was worried about you."

"Did you call the police?"

"I'm actually on my way down to the station in a bit. I thought it'd be easier to show them everything."

"Call me as soon as you get back. I'll be at Knead for a while."

"I will," he says. "And I'm sorry again. About everything."

"It's not your fault," I say, deciding not to tell him what happened with Ben.

We hang up, even though I can tell he wants to talk some more. I close my eyes again, trying to take Spencer's and Wes's advice to heart, to remind myself that I *am* human, that I'm bound to make mistakes, and that what's important is that I learn from them.

I just hope Ben feels the same.

# 49

*I* SPEND ANOTHER HOUR at Knead—wedging out my clay, forming it into shapes, and then smashing it back down against my work board. It's almost therapeutic.

That is, until I hear the pinging sound inside my head—the one from the alarm clock in Adam's car.

And so, I sculpt the clock, hoping that it may help make sense of why I'm hearing the noise in the first place. But sculpting it only makes the ringing louder, almost deafening, forcing me to clean up and head home.

It's late, so my parents don't really say too much or notice how fried-up-and-eaten I look. Mom just mutters something about how she and I need to talk tomorrow, and Dad complains about his yoga-aching back.

I escape to my room, wondering why Adam hasn't called me yet. I plug my cell phone into the charger and make a mental note to call him first thing in the morning.

Meanwhile, it feels like my body is shell-shocked. I reach for my comforter to lessen the chill. I take a sip of water to ease the dryness in my mouth. ChapStick for my cracked lips. Music to drown out my thoughts. The window open wide to allow the breeze to blow right through me—to make me feel awake, when every part of me feels tired, dead, numb.

But nothing seems to ease this ache. And I only feel colder, more confused, more isolated than in all my life. Still, I tell myself that I need to get some sleep. And then I lie down on my bed, hoping that exhaustion will take me.

My alarm clock goes off, startling me. I smack the snooze button, but it continues to blare—a high-pitched squeal that makes my head pound. I sit up in bed and yank the plug.

Still, it rings. And suddenly it dawns on me—it isn't my alarm clock at all. The ringing noise is inside my head.

*"When the clock bells chime,"* I whisper, remembering the twisted little jingle that played from the clown doll, and the time that flashed on the alarm clock.

Five o'clock. But obviously not five o'clock in the afternoon like we'd thought. Five o'clock in the morning.

Exactly thirty minutes from now.

I grab my cell and try Adam's number, but it goes straight to voice mail. I hop out of bed and pull on my coat, slip on some shoes, and tack a note up for my parents. I tell them I need to borrow the car for a friend-in-crisis emergency, and that I'll be back for breakfast.

The streets are dark and slick this morning. I end up skidding a couple of times, going way faster than I actually should. Finally, I get to Adam's apartment and park right out front, despite the sign warning me that I'll be towed.

The building looks especially eerie in the dark. The roads surrounding it are virtually still. I edge the car door open and enter the main lobby. The smell of something acidic—like cleaning fluid mixed with paint remover—smacks me in the face. I look around in search of the source, when a slamming noise startles me. I turn to find that the door has just shut behind me.

A clock on the wall tells me it's almost five o'clock. I quickly climb the stairs, tripping on the step at the very top. Now on Adam's floor, I go to his door and knock. I wait a couple of seconds before trying the knob. But it's locked. And he doesn't answer.

I try his cell number again. Still no luck.

I beat against his door with my fist, knowing he must be inside. Meanwhile, the alarm clock continues to ring inside my head—so loud that I almost have to cover my ears.

Finally, the door opens a crack.

Piper is there. "Oh, hi," she says, clearly embarrassed. She puts her hands up to cover the V-neck of her top, as if she were wearing something revealing, even though she's completely dressed. "Adam's still sleeping. We were up pretty late last night."

"So, I woke you?"

"Well, it *is* five a.m. on a Sunday morning."

"Oh," I say, noticing that she's wearing a fresh coat of lip gloss, and that her hair looks perfectly groomed.

"I really think you should go," she says; her voice is sharp.

"I just want to see Adam for a minute." I try to peek past her into the apartment, but she does her best to block my view.

"Don't you have your own boyfriend to worry about?" she asks.

"What's that supposed to mean?"

Piper starts to shut the door in my face, but I stop it with my foot.

"Go!" she insists. "Adam and I are busy."

"I thought you said you were sleeping."

At the same moment a clamoring sound comes from Adam's bedroom. I push my way past Piper and head in that direction, but she grabs my arm, attempting to hold me back.

"This is your last warning!" she barks.

I manage to pull away, but she snatches my arm again.

And cuts me.

Blood trickles from my forearm, through the sleeve of my jacket, dripping onto the rug. It takes me a moment to spot the knife in her hand. The handle is red, with an end that curls downward, and the tip is jagged.

It's just like the knife that Aunt Alexia painted.

I glance back at my arm, trying to stop the bleeding with my coat.

"Looking for more fun? Because it's too late to turn

back now." She comes at me with the knife again, but I'm able to dodge her by sticking my foot out at the right moment. She trips, falling to the floor with a thud.

I hurry into Adam's bedroom. He's tied to the bed. There's a strip of duct tape across his mouth. I hurry to his side, anxious to get him free.

A second later, Piper shoves me from behind and I go toppling onto the bed. "Against the headboard," she demands. "Place your hands where I can see them."

I do what she says, my mind scrambling over how to get us free.

"That's what you really want, isn't it?" she continues. "To be in my boyfriend's bed? To steal him away from me?"

"You've got it all wrong."

"Do I? So, you kiss all your friends like that?" She gestures toward the photo on Adam's night table. It sits on top of a stack of crossword puzzles. Apparently, he never went to the police after all. "The time is now," she continues, motioning to the alarm clock.

I can't quite tell if it's ringing or if the noise is still just inside my head. I look toward Adam's hands, bound at the wrists with duct tape and attached to the headboard.

"Impressed?" she asks, referring to her handiwork. "I drugged him while he slept. He woke up like this."

"You can't do this," I say, wondering if I can distract her—if, for just a second, I could reach into my pocket and call the police.

"Why not?" she asks. "Because you're here to save

him? Maybe that'll just make things more interesting."

"What are you talking about?"

"My plan was to give him an ultimatum," she explains. "Either he'd be with me in life, or he'd be with me in death. Of course, now that you're here, maybe you've been thinking about killing yourself, too. From what I hear, your life has been pretty depressing lately. It wasn't long ago that you were getting stalked as well. Adam told me all about it—about how your ex-boyfriend took candid snapshots of you, how he drugged you and tied you up in the back of some trailer. Tell me you're not still suffering from the repercussions of all that. Not to mention that your boyfriend broke up with you recently . . ."

"That's not true."

"Oh, no?" she asks, seemingly disappointed. "But he still must've been pretty upset, especially after seeing that photo. Maybe his disappointment was too much for you to handle."

"You don't know what you're talking about."

"What do *you* think, Adam? Is Camelia suicidal?"

"You're crazy," I whisper.

"You're right." She giggles. "I am. My shrink thinks so, too. She used to record our sessions together before she ended up dumping me. But you know what? It doesn't even matter. Because no one can help me. And so I've decided to help myself."

"And being with Adam will make things right? You'll still have issues."

"But he'll help me get through them. Adam is the best

thing that's ever happened to me, the only one who really gives a shit."

"Please," I insist, inching forward. "Let's get you some help."

"No!" she shouts, prompting me to scoot back again. "I don't need help." She slices the air with her knife.

Adam grunts a couple of times, as if he wants to talk. Keeping an eye on my hands, Piper orders me to remove the tape from his mouth. I take an end of the duct tape and peel it away.

Adam coughs before he's able to speak. "Please, just let Camelia go."

"It's too late for that," she says, tapping her palm with the blade. "You know what I think?" She narrows her eyes, looking at me. "I think that once you saw how close Adam and I were, you started feeling *really* depressed—so depressed that you decided to kill yourself."

"Just leave her out of this," Adam tells her. "I love you. I always have."

Piper's lip quivers. She seems taken aback by the words. "Then, prove it."

"Come over here," he says.

She hesitates. The tip of her knife cuts into the fabric of her jeans, but she doesn't even notice.

"Please," Adam says, angling his face as if he wants to kiss her.

She moves toward him, coming over to his side of the bed. Keeping her eyes locked on me, she places her lips over his mouth.

"Relax," he whispers, apparently sensing how weak the kiss is, how Piper isn't paying full attention.

She kisses him again, finally closing her eyes. Tears begin to course down her face.

A moment later, I dive at her, knocking her onto the floor. The knife shoots from her grip. I do my best to straddle her and pin her arms behind her, but she thrusts upward with her pelvis, and I go toppling off.

Piper struggles to reach the knife, a few feet away, in the corner of the room. I try to tug her back, grabbing at her shirt. She lets out a wail as I pull her hair.

She continues to move forward on her belly, toward the knife. I pounce on her back, trying to hold her in place, but she's still able to grab the knife by the blade.

"No!" I shout, hoping that someone can hear us—can hear our struggles, can hear Adam's sudden pleading with her to stop.

I scramble to my feet and hurry to the night table, in search of something—anything—to protect myself. I end up ripping the lamp right out of the wall, hoping I can use the heavy glass base as a weapon. Meanwhile, Adam continues to try to break free.

Piper comes at me with the knife. I thrust the lamp toward her head, but it smacks against her shoulder instead, and she merely staggers back as the lamp smashes against the floor.

She comes at me again, pressing me against the wall. My shoes slide on the broken glass. "You were so depressed," she whispers, pressing the tip of the knife against my neck. "When you found out that Adam was in love with me, you couldn't bear to live another day."

"No," I whimper, trying my best not to swallow.

"You cut your own throat with this knife."

"No!" Adam screams.

She presses the tip harder against my throat. I feel a trickle of blood roll down my neck. I try to think of something to say—anything that will finally get her to stop. Adam begs for her to come to her senses, insisting that he won't be with her if she doesn't.

I'm overcome with dizziness. My body weakens, and I feel myself start to falter.

At some point, Piper is pulled off of me.

I blink a couple of times. There's a swirl of gray around me as I slide down the wall, hearing her struggle.

It takes me a few moments to regain my breath, to be able to focus fully again.

That's when I see Ben.

Wearing gloves, he struggles to grab the knife from her, his hands clenching her wrists. The muscles in his forearms flex.

"Ben!" I shout, as Piper lets out a whine. For just a moment, I think he's going to break her wrists, but then he throws her onto the bed. She rolls off and hits the floor with a loud, hard smack. Blood gushes out her nose.

She gets back up and lunges at him, diving toward his midsection and throwing him backward onto the floor. On top of him now, she grabs the knife and drives it into his belly.

"No!" I hear myself scream. Ben lets out a wail that tears through my chest. I try to get up, but I stumble back.

Piper pulls the knife out of his belly.

Finally, I'm able to get up. My arm stings where she cut me, and my coat is stained with blood.

Piper holds the knife high above her head, ready to stab him again. The blade is as red as the handle now.

Just behind her, I muster up all the strength inside me and grab her arms, pulling them back. I squeeze the knife out of her grip. Piper jumps to her feet and swings at my head. Luckily, I'm able to dodge her and push her back. She goes down hard against Adam's dresser.

I grab my phone. My fingers trembling, it takes me a couple of tries to dial 9-1-1. I tell the operator to have the police come right away and to send an ambulance. And then I hang up, noticing that Ben isn't moving. It doesn't appear as if he's breathing, either.

# 50

$\mathcal{I}$ RUSH TO BEN'S SIDE and hover over his mouth, but I don't feel his breath. I breathe into his airway, trying to remember everything I learned in health class about resuscitation. Adam helps by talking me through it, ordering me to remain calm, to lift Ben's neck and apply pressure to his wound.

I shake my head, wondering what more I can do, and hear a ringing sound. At first I think it's the alarm clock still blaring in my ear, but then it dawns on me that it's the phone. I cut Adam free, and look toward Piper. She's passed out in the corner of the room.

Finally I answer the phone. It's the 9-1-1 operator, asking me all these questions about what happened. "He's been stabbed," I blurt. "He isn't breathing."

"Who's been stabbed?" the operator asks. "Where is the wound?"

"In his stomach." I cover my mouth at the sight of

him—at how unresponsive he is, at how blood has pooled all around him on the floor.

A moment later, I hear sirens. Soon, three police officers and a couple of paramedics come barging into the room. The medics go right into action on Ben, ordering me out of the way. They stick a ventilation mask over his face to try to get him breathing again.

"Please," I whisper, feeling my whole body tense.

The medics assess Ben's stab wound, place a dressing on it, and apply pressure. "He's lost a lot of blood," one of them says, starting an IV line.

"Is he going to be all right?" I ask.

No one answers. Meanwhile, a second group of medics comes in to assess Piper. They place her on a stretcher, though it seems she's regained consciousness. She glares at me.

*Will Ben be okay?* I scream inside my head, not sure whether the words actually come out. Part of me is afraid to know the answer.

The medics check Ben's level of alertness by asking him questions and examining his pupils. They recheck his oxygen mask to be sure he's breathing.

Finally, he is.

At some point, one of the medics notices my wounds. He starts to bandage me up, but I'm not really focused on me. I just can't stop looking at Ben.

"Will he be all right?" I ask again.

Still no answer.

Together, two medics lift Ben onto a stretcher. One of

them calls the hospital, stating what the situation is and that they're coming right away.

"Please," I insist. "Let me come, too."

The medic who bandaged my arm stares at me for about half a second, as if trying to decide. Finally, he agrees. Meanwhile, Piper is placed in a second ambulance. And Adam is taken to the police station to make a full report.

# 51

THE RIDE TO THE HOSPITAL goes by in a blur, sirens screaming, lights flashing. A heart that's almost stopped (mine).

But thankfully, Ben's keeps beating.

Once we arrive, a couple of nurses hold me back, insisting that I need to be checked out for any additional injuries.

"I'm fine," I tell them, literally dragging my feet along the linoleum flooring. "I just want to stay with Ben."

His face is pale. His eyes are peacefully shut.

Still, Ben and I are separated. While he's whisked off into another area entirely, I'm ushered into a crowded waiting area—at least fifty people are there—where the receptionist tells me to fill out some forms.

"You don't understand," I explain. More tears streak down my face. "My boyfriend was stabbed. I need to be with him."

But it's as if she doesn't hear me. She slides a clipboard full of forms at me. I reluctantly take them and begin to fill out my name, but when she isn't looking, I sneak away and head in the direction of where Ben was taken.

I start down a long corridor, peeking into rooms at the left and right, finally spotting the medic who tended to my wound. "Where's Ben?" I ask; my throat is sore and raw.

He hesitates, but then leads me around the corner and through a set of double doors. He gestures to a room at the very end and suggests that I take a seat on the bench outside it.

"No," I tell him. "I want to go in. I want to be with him."

"You can't go in. He's in critical condition."

"What does that mean?" I ask, desperate for a bit of clarity, for someone to be honest with me.

"Do you have his parents' contact information? Is there anyone who should know he's here?"

"Is he going to be okay?"

"You should call them," he says, ignoring my question. "You should get them down here right away."

"Why?" I ask.

The medic nods toward a bench and tells me to settle down.

"Not until I know if my boyfriend is going to be all right," I insist.

"Look," he says, softening slightly. "Your boyfriend was stabbed. He's in critical condition."

At the same moment, it dawns on me. The knife sculpture—and how I carved Ben's initials into the blade.

I rush to his room and turn the knob. But the medic holds me back as I kick, scream, and finally fall down at his feet.

"You don't understand!" I wail. "This is *my* fault. I should've known this would happen."

Before I can help it, I feel hands all over me as I'm dragged someplace else, still fighting, still kicking and screaming, and still begging for them to let me see Ben.

None of them listens, and it isn't long before the walls begin to crumble and fall around me, before everything goes black.

# 52

*I* WAKE UP AND SEE my parents first. They're sitting at my bedside. Mom wipes my forehead with a damp towel, and Dad asks if I want a drink of water. Layers of whiteness surround me: the walls, the ceiling, the blankets that cover me. "Where am I?" I whisper.

"Just relax," Mom says, tucking me in. "You're at the hospital. You passed out and you've been resting."

"Adam called us," Dad explains before I can ask. "He told us about what happened."

I sit up, noticing that I'm still in the same clothes. There are bandages around my arm and on my neck, and it's light outside the window. "Where's Ben?"

"Just relax," Mom insists, propping my pillow.

"It was *my* fault," I tell them. "I sculpted it. I should have known."

"You sculpted what?" she asks. Her face is a giant question mark.

I shake my head. It's too much to explain. "How long have I been asleep?"

"A little over an hour," Dad says.

"And how's Ben? Can I see him?"

Mom avoids the question by rearranging some stuff on my tray.

"Tell me," I insist, sitting up further. Every inch of me feels bruised. "How is he?"

"He's lost a lot of blood," Dad says. "He's still in critical condition."

"Meaning he's not conscious?"

"Not yet," he says, squeezing my hand.

I look at my mom, but she gets up and stands away from the bed so I can't see her face.

"I need to see him," I plead.

"You can't see him," Dad says. "Only family members are allowed in right now. His aunt is with him. His parents are on their way."

"What you need is to come home," Mom says, regaining her composure. She turns to face me again.

"No," I say, refusing to leave. "I need to be here for him. I need to be here when he wakes up."

A moment later, there's a knock on the door. A nurse comes in with Kimmie and Wes. Kimmie comes over and wraps her arms around me. Apparently, Adam called her, too.

"It'll be okay," she tells me.

I want to believe her. But if Ben doesn't wake up, nothing will ever be okay again.

My parents continue to insist that I come home. The nurse tells me that I should get some rest, too. "You've been through a lot," the nurse says.

"No," I whisper, still refusing to leave. "I'm not going anywhere without Ben."

"We'll stay with her," Kimmie tells my parents. "We'll make sure she has something to eat—"

"And doesn't take down any more hospital staff," Wes jokes.

While they continue to discuss what to do with me, I get up, splash some water on my face, and promise my parents that I'll call them later.

"I'll stay, too," Dad says. He gives Mom the keys and tells her to go home and get some rest. Her eyes are blood-shot, and she looks as if she hasn't slept in days.

It takes some convincing, but Mom finally agrees, especially when Dad promises to text her with hourly updates.

While he paces the length of the corridor, I head out to the bench by Ben's room to wait. Later, Dad offers me something cold to drink. Kimmie urges me to try eating a sandwich she's brought from the cafeteria. Wes gets me a blanket. They give me magazines to read.

But all I want to do is sit here and wait until Ben comes to.

At one point, a police officer shows up and asks me a battery of questions about what happened with Piper.

Soon after, Adam comes to check on things, to offer more help, and to inquire about Ben.

And then I wait some more.

About two hours later, with Dad snoozing on the bench beside us, Ben's aunt finally comes out of Ben's room.

"How's he doing?" I ask, standing up.

She shakes her head. "I don't have a good feeling."

"Why?" I ask. Tears fill my eyes again. "Can I see him?"

Ben's aunt agrees to this and lets me inside the room.

He's hooked up to all kinds of machines that are keeping him alive. A monitor beeps to the rhythm of his heartbeat. I sit by his bed and pull the covers over him. In doing so, I accidentally brush against his thigh.

And that's when I feel it.

That same electrical sensation I got the first time I touched the spot—in my room, when I begged him to stay the night. The feeling radiates up my spine and gnaws at my nerves. It's like something's there, marked on his leg.

I run my fingers over the spot—through the blanket— almost tempted to have a look. I close my eyes, trying to sense things the way he does—to get a mental picture from merely touching the area. But I can't. And I don't.

Still, I have to know if I'm right.

I peer over my shoulder toward the door, checking to see that no one's looking in. And then I roll the covers down.

Ben's wearing a hospital gown. With trembling fingers, I pull up the hem and see it right away: the image of a chameleon, tattooed on his upper thigh. It's about four inches long, with green and yellow stripes.

And its tail curls into the letter *C*.

I feel my face furrow, wondering when he got the tattoo, and why he never told me. It wasn't so long ago that I told him the story of my name—how my mother named me after a chameleon, because chameleons have keen survival instincts.

"You'll survive this as well," I whisper.

I roll the covers back up over him and take his hand, noticing how well our palms fit together and thinking back to just after the last time he saved me—when he took my hand and told me that we'd always be together.

I lower my head to his chest and continue to squeeze his palm. Tears fall onto the bedsheets, dampening the fabric just above his heart. "I'm so sorry," I tell him, over and over again.

A few moments later, there's a twitching sensation inside my hand. Ben's finger glides over my thumb. "Sorry for what?" he breathes. His voice is raspy and weak.

I lift my head to check his face. His eyelids flutter. The monitor starts beeping faster. And his lips struggle to move.

"Don't try to talk," I tell him, searching for the nurse's call buzzer.

"Please," he whispers, his eyes almost fully open now. "Don't let go."

"I won't," I promise, gripping his hand even harder.

I T WASN'T LONG before Ben was moved into recovery. The police came in to talk to him, ordering me out of the room, even when I begged them to let me stay.

Eventually, I was ordered to leave the hospital altogether. Ben's nurses told me that I needed to go home and get some rest if my own wounds were going to heal.

To my surprise, Ben agreed.

"Are you sure?" I asked him.

He nodded and looked away, as if, the stronger and more conscious he got, the more he was able to remember.

It's been a full week since that happened. Ben is home now. But he hasn't been returning my calls.

I've been trying not to dwell on it, to give him the space that he needs, and to catch up on some much-needed rest. But now I feel ready to tie up some of the loose ends.

First on my agenda: I draft a letter to my aunt, telling her that I know she isn't crazy, that I have a feeling I know exactly what she's going through, and that somehow I'll see to it that she gets out of that hospital and into the hands of people who can really help her—people who know about extrasensory powers.

Like the one I obviously have.

I seal the envelope, wishing I'd been able to decipher the knife sculpture I did—that I'd stopped and questioned the fact that I'd carved Ben's initials into the blade. Maybe then I could've warned him. Maybe then he could've avoided any impending dangerous situations.

Though I know deep down that wouldn't have mattered to him; he would've come to save me anyway. Which is one of the things I love most about him.

I take the letter to the mailbox at the end of my street, feeling a giant sense of relief as I feed it through the slot. Back in the house, Mom emerges from the family room, having finished her morning meditation. She's still in her pajamas; there are tiny Buddha figures patterned across the flannel fabric.

"We need to talk," I say, before she can even utter a "good morning."

"I'm glad to hear you're ready." She sits down at the kitchen island. "Your father and I wanted to give you some time to process everything."

"Well, thanks," I say, taking a seat across from her.

"So, I think we should talk about trust," she begins. "I want you to feel that you can trust your dad and me, no matter what. Even if you don't think we'll agree with you. I speak for the both of us when I say that we're proud of you for wanting to help out a friend, but you have to admit, you were in way over your head."

"I do admit it," I say, nodding as she tells me that I should've told them what was going on, that it was wrong of me not to go to the police, and that there are trained professionals at Adam's school whose job it is to deal with this type of thing.

"We're on the same team," she reminds me.

"I know. And I do trust you and Dad."

"Really?" Her eyes narrow. "Because I feel like we've been through this before."

"I know," I repeat. "I just thought that I could handle it all." As stupid as that might sound.

"Look, I don't want to lecture you," she continues. "I just want you to feel like you can come to me about things."

"And you need to do the same."

Mom gets up to fill the kettle with water for tea. "You're obviously talking about Aunt Alexia."

"I think she should come and stay with us for a while." I raise my voice over the running faucet. "It's not like we don't have a spare bedroom."

She turns off the water and shoots me a curious look. "You've obviously been talking to Dad about this."

"*Dad?*" I ask.

"It's just that he suggested the same." She reaches for her bottle of pills, but doesn't open it.

*"Seriously?"* I ask, completely taken aback, especially since Aunt Alexia's drama has been at the root of some of their problems.

Instead of pursuing the conversation, Mom starts prattling about the merits of green tea versus red and white, then confesses that she doesn't want to make a rash decision about Aunt Alexia's therapy. "I just worry that it might be too difficult with her here. I wouldn't want her to have another outburst like the one at the hospital."

"I don't think she will," I say, fairly confident that, if Alexia were given the appropriate channels to discuss her touch power—treating it as a gift rather than a curse—things would start to improve. "I'm just surprised that it was Dad's idea."

"Your dad said it might be good for you." She pours us a couple of mugs of tea. "I didn't really understand it myself, but he's convinced that you two are kindred spirits of some sort . . . with your art and with how intense you both can be."

I force a smile, to mask my shock, wondering if Dad's suggestion was truly sincere. Or if he might know a whole lot more than he's actually letting on.

Back in my room, I reach for my cell phone, anxious to call Kimmie. She's been an amazing friend during this whole ordeal, calling to check on me daily and dropping by with non-raw-food goodness in the form of chicken soup and salty french fries.

She picks up on the first ring and tells me that she and

Wes are on their way over. Not five minutes later, they're at my front door.

"I hope you don't mind that we're crashing," Wes says. "I'm trying to escape a hunting expedition. No joke. Dad thinks I'll be more of a man if I can blow a rabbit's head off. And my response? *'Sorry, Dad, but as tempting as it is to obliterate Peter Cottontail first thing on a Sunday morning, I promised Camelia I'd swing by her house, because she's been begging to abuse my body for weeks.'*"

"And speaking of being delusional," Kimmie segues, "did I mention that my plan to reunite my parents was totally dumb?" She leads us into my bedroom and then closes the door behind her. "They could smell the setup before their water glasses were even filled."

"How's that?" I ask, taking a seat on my bed.

"The violinist I arranged to serenade them at the table might have been a tip-off," she begins. "Either that, or the wrist corsage I ordered for my mom. I handpicked the begonias and had the florist deliver it right to the table."

"Don't forget about the oyster appetizer you preordered for the occasion," Wes adds.

"Because, you know what they say about oysters, right?" An evil grin breaks out across her face. "I know, I know." She sighs, before I can even say anything. "I may have gone a little overboard, but what can I say? I'm a *dorkus extremus*. Hence my outfit du jour." She's wearing a Catholic schoolgirl's uniform, a pair of clunky black glasses (with the requisite amount of tape on the bridge), and a cone-shaped dunce cap.

"Yes, but you're a *dorkus extremus* with a nice set of begonias," Wes teases.

Kimmie shrugs and sits beside me on the bed, resting her head against my shoulder. The point of her dunce cap extends behind my neck. "Anyway, they had a huge talk with me last night, telling me that they're both actually happier on their own, and that I need to start getting used to that idea."

"And so, what do you think?" I ask, glad to finally be able to reciprocate her friendship.

"I don't know. I mean, what does *happy* have to do with anything? We're talking about their responsibility as parents here."

"And do you honestly feel like they were better parents before all this?"

Kimmie lifts her head, as if a lightbulb just went on somewhere inside it—as if it were pretty darned clear what the correct answer is.

"So what about *your* dating drama?" She bumps Wes's knee with the toe of her saddle shoe, obviously darting my question. "Are you and Tiffany Bunkin history?"

"Ancient," he says. "I mean, she's cute and sweet and thoughtful and all that. . . . I guess it's just really hard to explain."

"And what's the story with Ben?" Kimmie asks me. "Or is that subject still taboo?"

"Not taboo, just mysterious."

"Like, the whole key issue?" Wes asks. "What was up with that? How was Piper able to get into Adam's apartment all those times?"

"The police had the same question."

"And?"

"And she had her own key. She was around his place so often that she swiped Adam's spare set—the set formerly used by his ex-roommate. She made a copy for herself and then returned the keys before Adam ever knew they were gone."

"Well, the good thing is that Ben saved you," he says. "I mean, he obviously still really cares about you."

"I know," I say, confident that he does, but still not sure that's enough.

"So, what's going to happen to Piper?" Kimmie asks.

"I'm not really sure."

After the arrest, Piper's parents came forward, surprisingly unfazed by all she'd done. Apparently, she's been in therapy since she was a kid, but, as she told Adam and me, no one was able to help her. That was the one honest thing she said. The rest were lies, including all the stories she supposedly told Adam and her therapist about being abused by her dad as a kid.

"Will Adam press charges?" Wes asks.

"I doubt it," I say, remembering how Piper's parents offered to pay for any mental and/or physical damage any of us incurred as a result of their daughter's "*disillusion*." But, like Adam, I'm not looking for any monetary compensation. "I just want to get my life back on track," I tell them. I brush my fingers over my mouth, reminded of Adam's kiss. And then I gaze into the center of my palm, still able to feel Ben's grip on my hand.

# 54

I SPEND THE NEXT SEVERAL days going through the motions at school, but, like Ben, I avoid the social scene at all costs. He's back at school as well, but we haven't really been talking much, just giving each other polite nods in passing.

I've been spending most of my free time at Knead, delving into my pottery and finally taking Spencer's advice about using my emotion as a springboard to great work.

"Think of your suffering as a gift," he reminds me. "What I wouldn't give to have a girlfriend cheat on me with an ex-best friend, only to wind up as an almost-victim in a mass suicide. Inspiration like that doesn't come around like candy."

"Not funny," I tell him, knowing he's not being insensitive; he's just trying to make me laugh.

I dip my sponge into a bin of water, thinking about how Adam's been trying to cheer me up as well. Like

Kimmie, he's been calling me on a regular basis and cracking his usual corny jokes. He even made me a crossword puzzle that said, IT'S GONNA BE A BRIGHT, SUNSHINY DAY and drew a cartoon version of Johnny Nash on the envelope.

It almost got a giggle out of me. *Almost.*

The other night, he stopped by my house to bring me a cup of café mocha and a vanilla-bean scone from the Press & Grind. He stood at my front door and told me that whatever I needed—and whenever I needed it—he'd be there for me. "And not as payback," he explained, "but because I really care about you. Don't ever forget that." He stared into my eyes for a moment too long, perhaps waiting for me to say the same.

But instead I simply told him that I wouldn't forget it. To my surprise—and disappointment (because I wished I could've returned the sentiment)—he left shortly after.

While Spencer and Svetlana glaze cereal bowls in the back room, I continue to work on my own bowl, noticing that it looks like two lovers embracing. The sculpture is tall, more vaselike than bowl-like when it comes right down to it, and the sides are curved, resembling entangled limbs. I started the project the day before yesterday, and I've been working on it since then, just seeing where my impulse takes me.

Like with Ben.

It turns out that he knew where to find me that morning—when Piper tied Adam up and gave him that deadly ultimatum—by touching the kiss photo. It still carried

Piper's vibe. Apparently, he'd held it for a good part of the night—until he could practically hear the alarm buzzing, too.

He called me a little while ago, asking if we could talk once and for all. I look up toward the entrance when I hear the doorbell chime his arrival.

"Hey," he says, coming right over to take a peek at my work. Despite the accident, he looks better than ever: a sweatshirt that's snug at the chest, helmet-disheveled hair, and a subtle glow to his skin.

"How are you feeling?" I ask.

He pats his wound. "Getting better, and you?" He gestures at my arm and then gazes at my neck.

I nod, telling him that I'd like to lie low for a bit, take a break from playing Supergirl. "At least for a little while." I smirk.

"Adam was lucky to have you," he says.

"Well, we were both lucky to have *you*."

Ben shrugs. "I still feel pretty weird about it. When I pushed Piper, I never expected for her to go flying like that."

"She tumbled off the bed," I say, correcting him.

"And broke her nose. She landed pretty hard against the floor."

"She tried to kill you," I remind him.

"And if you hadn't have been there, she would've. So, thanks."

I shake my head, knowing that if it hadn't been for me, Ben wouldn't have been there in the first place. I try to tell him that, but he swats my words away with his hand and says he wants to show me something.

"Sure," I say, wondering if he's really as nervous as he seems.

He clenches his teeth and hesitates a couple of moments; the angles of his face seem to grow sharper. Finally, he motions to the pant leg of his jeans.

There's a tear right over his thigh.

"I know you saw it in the hospital," he says, exposing the chameleon tattoo through the torn fabric. "I felt you . . . looking at it. Anyway, I wanted you to know that I did this back home, before I ever came to Freetown. Before I ever met you."

"So it's a coincidence?"

His dark gray eyes swallow mine whole. "Do you honestly believe that?"

"No," I say, listening as he proceeds to tell me that a few months before he got to town, he touched his mother's wedding band—something that reminded him of soul mates—and the image of a chameleon stuck inside his head.

"I couldn't get it out of my mind," he explains. "It was almost like the image was welded to my brain, behind my eyes, haunting me even when I tried to sleep."

"And you got the tattoo because of that?"

"Because I hoped its permanence might help me understand it more—might help me understand what it had to do with my own soul mate."

"And do you understand it now?" I ask, swallowing hard.

"Yeah." He smiles. "I suppose I do."

I take a deep breath, trying to hold myself together, desperate to know what he's truly trying to say here, and what I should say to him as well. I close my eyes, picturing that moment in the hospital when I held his hand and wondering if he would've recovered as quickly if it hadn't been for the connection between us—the electricity he must have sensed from my touch.

"But I think I still need time," he says.

I nod, almost relieved that he said it first. "Yeah, me too."

Ben's lips tremble ever so slightly, surprised by my response maybe. "But I want you to know that you're not the only one to blame here," he says. "You wouldn't have kissed Adam if I hadn't given you a reason to. I could sense how insecure you were. I didn't do anything to change that."

"You didn't take advantage of it, either," I say, thinking back to that time in my room, when I begged him to stay the night.

"Someday you'll see that we both played a part."

"And someday *you'll* see that you weren't the only one keeping secrets." I bite my lip, thinking how I wasn't completely open about everything, either.

There's silence between us for several moments, just the buzzing of the overhead lights and Svetlana giggling in the back room. I look down at my sculpture, suddenly feeling more vulnerable than I ever thought possible.

"I've missed you," he says, following my gaze. "Even

before all that stuff went down. . . . I've missed the way things were between us." He reaches out to touch the rim of my sculpture, making me feel even more exposed, as if he can sense how suddenly swollen I feel, or the aching deep inside me.

"Maybe it can be that way again someday," I tell him.

Ben nods and takes a step back, as if what he senses is all too much. His eyes are as broken as mine now.

"But first you have to forgive me," I continue.

He comes around to my side of the table, takes my hands, and brushes his lips against my forehead. "And you have to forgive me, too."

My heart pounds, and blood rushes to my ears, making me feel a little dizzy. I'm so tempted to ask him to stay, but I also know what's best for me. And right now, that means taking some time out for myself.

I pull away, breaking his clasp on my hands, no longer willing to share all my thoughts with him. Instead, I tell him that he'll always be a part of my life, and then I let him go.

## Acknowledgments

Many thanks to my former editor Jennifer Besser. It was a thrill and an honor to work with you. Thanks so much for your editorial guidance, your contagious enthusiasm, and for always knowing just the right questions to ask. You helped make me a better writer.

A special thanks to my editor Christian Trimmer. Your careful eye, critical suggestions, and keen sense of story have helped make my work stronger. I've already learned so much from you.

Thanks to my agent Kathryn Green for her invaluable advice and guidance, and to all the friends and family members who have supported me, offered to read my pages-in-progress, and pitched in to give me time to write (you know who you are).

And lastly, a great big thank-you goes to my readers for their continuous support, boundless enthusiasm, and amazing generosity. I'm so very truly grateful.

Look for the next book
in the Touch series,
**DEADLY LITTLE VOICES**

# DEADLY LITTLE VOICES

*A* VOICE STARTLES ME AWAKE. It's a female voice with a menacing tone, and it whispers into my ear.

And tells me that I should die.

I sit up in bed and click on my lamp. It's 4:10 a.m. My bedroom door is closed. The window is locked. The curtains are drawn. And I'm alone.

*I'm alone.*

So, then, why can't I shake this feeling—this sensation that I'm being watched?

I draw up the covers and tell myself that the voice was part of a dream. I remember my dream distinctly. I dreamt that I was in my pottery studio, using a spatula to perfect a sculpture I've been working on: a figure skater with her arms crossed over her chest and her leg extended back. I began the sculpture just a few days ago, but I haven't touched it since.

I look down at my hands, noticing how I can almost feel a lingering sensation of clay against my fingertips.

That's how real the dream felt.

I take a deep breath and lie back down. But the voice comes at me again—in my ear, rushing over my skin, and sending chills straight down my back.

Slowly, I climb out of bed and cross the room, wondering if maybe there's someone else here. Standing in front of my closet door, I can feel my heart pound. I take another step and move to turn the knob.

At the same moment, a voice cries out: a high-pitched squeal that cuts right through my bones. I steel myself and look around the room.

Finally, I find the source: two eyes stare up at me from a pile of clothes on the floor. I'd recognize those eyes anywhere. Wide and green, they belong to my old baby doll, from when I was six.

She has twisty long blond hair like mine and a quarter-inch-long gash in her rubber cheek.

I haven't seen the doll in at least ten years.

Ten years since I lost her.

Ten years since my dad scoured every inch of the house looking for her and, when he couldn't, offered to buy me a new one.

My arms shaking, I pick up the doll, noticing the black X's drawn on her ears. I squeeze her belly and she cries out again, reminding me of a wounded bird.

I rack my brain, desperate for some sort of logical explanation, wondering if maybe this isn't my doll at all.

If maybe it's just a creepy replica. I mean, how can a doll that's been missing for ten years suddenly just reappear? But when I flip her over to check her back, I see that logic doesn't have a place here.

Because this doll is definitely mine.

The star is still there—the one I inked above the hem of her shorts when I became fascinated by the idea of all things astrological.

I pinch my forearm so hard the skin turns red. I'm definitely awake. My backpack is slumped at the foot of my bed, where I left it last night. The snapshot of Dad and me in front of the tree this past Christmas is still pasted up on my dresser mirror.

Aside from the doll, everything appears as it should.

So, then, how is this happening?

In one quick motion, I whisk my closet door open and pull the cord that clicks on the light. My clothes look normal, my shoes are all there, my last year's Halloween costume (a giant doughnut, oozing with creamy filling—a lame attempt to rebel against my mother's vegan ways) is hanging on a back hook, just as it should be.

Meanwhile, the voice continues. It whispers above my head, behind my neck, and into the inner recesses of my ear. And tells me that I'm worthless as a human being.

I open my bedroom door and start down the hallway, to go and find my parents. But with each step, the voice gets deeper, angrier, more menacing. It tells me how ugly I look, how talentless I am, and how I couldn't be more pathetic.

"You're just one big, fat joke," the voice hisses. The words echo inside my brain.

I cover my ears, but still the insults keep coming. And suddenly I'm six years old again with my doll clenched against my chest and a throbbing sensation at the back of my head.

I look toward my parents' closed bedroom door, feeling my stomach churn. I reach out to open their door, but I can't seem to find it now. There's a swirl of colors behind my eyes, making me dizzy. I take another step, holding the wall to steady myself; the floor feels like it's tilting beneath my feet.

On hands and knees now, I close my eyes to ease the ache in my head.

"Just do it," the voice whispers. It's followed by more voices, of different people. All trapped inside my head. The voices talk over one another and mingle together, producing one clear-cut message: that I'm a waste of a life. Finally, I find the knob and pull the door open, but my palms brush against a wad of fabric, and I realize that I haven't found my parents' bedroom after all.

It's the hallway closet. A flannel sheet tumbles onto my face.

Instead of turning away, I crawl inside and crouch on the floor, praying for the voices to stop.

But they only seem to get louder.

I rock back and forth, trying to remain in control. I smother my ears with the sheet. Press my forehead against my knees. Pound my heels into the floor, bracing myself for whatever's coming next.

Meanwhile, there's a drilling sensation inside my head; it pushes through the bones of my skull, and makes me feel like I'm going crazy.

"Please," I whisper. More tears sting my eyes. I shake my head, wondering if maybe I'm already dead, if maybe the voices are part of hell.

Finally, after what feels like forever, the words in my head start to change. A voice tells me that I'm not alone.

"I'm right here with you," the voice says, in a tone that's soft and serene.

An icy sensation encircles my forearm and stops me from rocking. I open my eyes and pull the sheet from my face, and am confused by what I see.

The hallway light is on now. A stark white hand is wrapped around my wrist. It takes me a second to realize that the hand isn't my own. The fingers are soiled with a dark red color.

Aunt Alexia is crouching down in front of me. Her green eyes look darker than usual, the pupils dilated, and the irises filled with broken blood vessels. Her pale blond hair hangs down at the sides of her face, almost like a halo.

"Am I dead?" I ask, rubbing at my temples, wondering if the red on her hands is from a gash in my head.

"Shhh," she says, silencing the other voices completely.

"Am I dead?" I repeat. My throat feels like it's bleeding, too.

She shakes her head. A smear of red lingers on my forearm. I see now that it's paint. "Come with me," she whispers.

I blink a couple of times to make sure she's really here—that she's not some apparition straight out of my dream. Dressed in a paint-spattered T-shirt and a pair of torn jeans, Aunt Alexia leads me out of the closet and back into my room. She helps me into bed, taking care to tuck my doll in beside me. And then she starts humming a whimsical tune—something vaguely familiar, from childhood, maybe. Her lips are the color of dying red roses.

I pinch myself yet again to confirm I'm not dreaming. The time on my clock reads 4:43.

"Has it really only been a half hour?" I ask, thinking aloud.

Aunt Alexia doesn't answer. Instead she continues to hum to me. Her voice reminds me of flowing water, somehow easing me to sleep.